The Last Flight
of the Birdman

The *Last Flight* of the *Birdman*

DAVE GLAZE

to Renlee –
my friend from
Brevoort Park!
Dave Glaze
Oct 15, 2007

COTEAU
BOOKS
FOR KIDS

Edited by Barbara Sapergia.
Cover images – *models*: Denique LeBlanc, by Paul Austring and "Young girl, portrait" by Digital Vision Photography; *plane*: "Bob St. Henry airborne over Saskatoon August, 1911 – Aviation Pioneers of Saskatchewan." Sask Arts Board print R-A 9618 - 4.
Cover montage and design by Duncan Campbell.
Book design by Duncan Campbell and Karen Steadman.
Printed and bound in Canada by Marquis Bookprinting Inc.

Library and Archives Canada Cataloguing in Publication

Glaze, Dave, 1947-
    Last flight of the Birdman / Dave Glaze.
(1912: The Mackenzie Davis files ; 2)

ISBN 978-1-55050-373-9
1. Saskatoon (Sask.)—Juvenile fiction. I. Title. II. Series:
Glaze, Dave, 1947- 1912: The Mackenzie Davis files ; 2.

PS8563.L386L38 2007   jC813'.54   C2007-904588-X

10 9 8 7 6 5 4 3 2 1

2517 Victoria Ave.
Regina, Saskatchewan
Canada S4P 0T2

Available in Canada & the US from
Fitzhenry & Whiteside
195 Allstate Parkway
Markham, ON, L3R 4T8

The publisher gratefully acknowledges the financial support of its publishing program by: the Saskatchewan Arts Board, the Canada Council for the Arts, the Government of Canada through the Book Publishing Industry Development Program (BPIDP), and the City of Regina Arts Commission.

*To the professional and volunteer historians,
archivists, librarians and museum workers
of Saskatchewan.*

The Daily Phoenix

FRIDAY, AUGUST 2, 1912

FAMOUS AVIATOR TO FLY AT SASKATOON FAIR

Biplane Will Arrive on Flatcar

One of the thrilling features of next week's Saskatoon Fair will be the finest exhibition of aerial navigation ever seen in western Canada. Birdman Glenn L. Martin is one of the best-known fliers in the United States and holds many records for distance and height in the young and daring field of aviation. Although dozens of brave men and not a few women have joined Mr. Martin in the skies, many of these aviators have fallen from the clouds and lost their lives in the pursuit of their dreams.

Mr. Martin's biplane, which he designed himself, has been dismantled and fitted into special crates which are being transported by rail to Saskatoon. When he reaches the city, the Birdman and his mechanic will assemble the aeroplane and prepare it for flight. On Monday, August 5, the day before the Exhibition opens, the aviator has promised to make an exciting journey from the fairgrounds to the city and back across the river.

CHAPTER ONE
Monday, August 5, 1912

MACKENZIE FOUND THE SPACE ALBERT HAD somehow saved for him in the knots of people jammed shoulder to shoulder along the walkway. Smiling, he flattened himself against the warm iron railing beside his friend. The narrow Traffic Bridge over the South Saskatchewan River was packed with motor cars and horse-drawn buggies and wagons, none of them moving. The whole sweltering throng stood searching the clear prairie sky.

"Great spot," Mackenzie said. "Thanks."

"Five more minutes," Albert grumbled. "If he's not here by then, I'm leaving." Like Mackenzie, Albert wore a floppy tweed hat and a white shirt too frayed for school. His dark trousers barely reached the tops of his scuffed boots. Reaching into his pocket for a small handful of coins, he added, "I'm running more errands for my father so I'll have money for the Fair. Then I'm going to the Roller Rink. You should come, Mack. It's free this week because it just opened."

"I'm sure he's already in the air," Mackenzie said, shielding his eyes from the sun with the peak of his cap. He glanced up a girder high above the two lanes of traffic. Four young men sat with their feet dangling below the beam. One of them pointed to where the river disappeared around a turn in the valley. Mackenzie stared over the water.

"There!" the man pointing cried. "The Birdman! He's coming straight toward us."

"I see him! I see him!" another man shouted.

A black speck about the size of an insect drifted toward the bridge. As Mackenzie watched, the bug grew larger. Soon it sprouted a double set of wings, like those of a dragonfly. The Birdman!

"How did he get over there?" someone asked. "He was supposed to take off from the Exhibition Grounds."

"He did. It's because he's so high. You lose sight of him."

"He goes up thousands of feet."

"Thousands? Surely not."

"He says he'll try for a new record while he's here. The highest a man has ever flown in Canada, a mile or more."

"That's not possible!"

The biplane veered west toward downtown where every office building seemed to have people standing on its rooftop and hanging from its upper windows.

The aeroplane's engine and its giant propeller rested on the lower cloth-covered wing just behind where Mr. Martin sat on a small seat. His boots were propped on footrests and his hands gripped what looked like an automobile's steering wheel. Smaller wings were fastened to poles that reached far to the front and back of the craft. Below hung three wheels looking like feet ready to touch the ground.

Waves of cheers arose when the biplane left downtown. He sees us! Mackenzie thought. He must. He's coming our way.

As it neared the river, the thum-thum-thum of the biplane's engine sent a shiver through the swarm on the bridge. It sounds just like a motor car, Mackenzie thought. Two horses harnessed to a buggy near the boys swung their heads together to share nervous looks.

Mr. Martin smiled toward his audience, lifted his left hand from the wheel, and waved.

The crowd gasped. Mackenzie clenched the railing.

The Birdman released his right hand and held both arms over his head.

"The fool! Look at him. Does he not see where he's heading?"

"He's going to crash into the bank."

Don't, Mackenzie pleaded. Go higher. Higher!

"No, he's going to make it. He did it. See? There he goes."

Like an eagle gliding without a beat of its wings,

the craft floated out of sight over the tops of the river-bank trees. The multitude applauded.

"Well, I never," someone exclaimed as the crowd on the walkway shuffled to form two rows, one going in each direction.

"Wasn't that incredible?" Mackenzie exclaimed, joining the line toward downtown. "He made it look easy to fly. I wonder what he'll do at the grandstand tomorrow?"

"Just like he did today," Albert said. "He'll go up and down, left and right. It's not that fabulous."

"Wouldn't you like to fly like the Birdman? I would."

"No. When I'm old enough, I'm going to have one of those." Albert nodded toward a driver stepping out of his motor car. The man walked to the front of the automobile, inserted a bent steel shaft into a slot, and looked over his shoulder.

"Hold onto your horses!" The driver watched men around him tighten their grips on their team's bridles then spun the crank. He pulled out the shaft and climbed back into his vehicle.

"Now that would be exciting," Albert said as the automobile belched a puff of smoke and putt-putted off the bridge.

"Are you coming roller skating with me?" he asked.

"I've never done it before."

"It's easy," Albert said. "It's just like ice-skating. You're good at that."

"I have to pick up my father's shirts from the laundry."

"That won't take long. Or are you going to be visiting with that Chinaman kid? Why do you spend so much time with him?"

"There's nothing wrong with Jin. I like him."

"Your parents let you?"

"Sure. Why wouldn't they?"

"Those Chinamen aren't the same as us, Mack. They'll get you into trouble."

Albert's doing it again, Mackenzie thought, complaining about anybody who isn't just like him. But Jin isn't that different. He doesn't look the same, but that's all. He's still my friend. "Jin isn't going to get me into any trouble."

Albert pointed to the roller skating rink that sat like an upended barrel on the downtown side of the river. "I'll be waiting for you there in twenty minutes," he said. "You'll like it, Mack. You strap on some roller skates, and in no time flat I'll teach you how to *really* fly."

LEE'S LAUNDRY was a small white-boarded building nestled in the midst of Saskatoon's Chinatown between the Traffic Bridge and the Canadian Northern Railway Bridge. A bell jangled when Mackenzie opened the door. The air inside was hot, heavy with the bad-egg smell of cheap coal, and wet like the fog that some days would hang over the river.

5

A counter ran from one side of the building to the other. Further back, faded green curtains hid the washing area from view. In between the counter and the curtains sat two tables and a simmering stove. Blankets and a sheet had been drawn tightly over each table and nailed to the underside. On the scrubbed-steel stovetop, a collection of irons rested like a flock of baby ducks. From a dusty window high in the front wall, brownish sunlight streamed across the room and coloured a white shirt flattened over one of the tables.

Mr. Lee walked out from behind the curtains. Dressed in a black suit and white shirt and tie, the old man met Mackenzie at the counter.

"Hello, Mr. Lee." Mackenzie held out a small square of red paper marked in black ink with a Chinese character. "I'm here for my father's shirts. Did you see the aeroplane flying over?"

"Yes," Mr. Lee said, taking the paper. "Jin called me to look. It is very noisy, like a big bumblebee floating in the air." He turned to a wall lined with rows of shelves holding bundles wrapped in brown paper marked with Chinese characters and tied with string. "It flew toward the river," he said, "but I do not know if it made it across."

"He did! Mr. Martin was going to fly all the way to the Exhibition Grounds."

Mr. Lee handed Mackenzie a package and reached under the counter for a hand-sized notebook with a worn brown cover. Flipping to a page, he picked up a pencil and wrote quickly. "Okay," he said, "Mr. Davis will pay at the end of the month." Closing the notebook, he asked, "Will it fly tomorrow?"

"He'll come back over the city, Mr. Lee. He might go really high, up into the clouds, so far he'll go right out of sight."

Chuckling, Mr. Lee said, "That is too high for me. Tell Jin. Tell Jin about this bumblebee that flies so high."

"Is he here?"

"Yes. Jin is filling the bags." He turned to call over his shoulder in Chinese.

That sounds like singing, Mackenzie thought as Jin replied. I wonder what they're saying.

"Jin works very hard," Mr. Lee said. "Very, very hard." Then, "When the bags are ready, Jin will meet you outside."

"Thank you," Mackenzie said.

Mr. Lee walked to the stove and picked up an iron. Licking the tip of his finger, he touched it to the bottom to see how hot the iron was and carried it to where the shirt lay waiting.

SITTING IN THE SHADE between the laundry and the Chinese rooming house next door, Mackenzie guided the blade of his jackknife along the edge of a hand-sized block of cedar. Flicking away a sliver of the wood, he turned the piece in his hand and, being careful not to cut too deeply, peeled off another slice.

When he heard the back door of the laundry slap shut, Mackenzie picked up his parcel and scrambled to his feet. A moment later Jin arrived, hauling two green cloth bags that hung from the ends of a six-foot pole balanced on his left shoulder. As usual, Jin was wearing baggy blue clothes that looked like pyjamas and sandals that flopped against his heels when he walked. Mackenzie wondered if those were the only clothes Jin owned. Unlike Mackenzie's trim cut, Jin's straight black hair hid his forehead and fell over his ears.

"Where are you going with those?" Mackenzie asked, pocketing the knife and piece of wood. "Are they heavy? They must hurt your shoulder."

"Not too heavy," Jin said. "It is uniforms for the Lucky Star Café."

"Pass them here," Mackenzie said.

"You want to carry this? Why? You should be happy to walk without such a load."

"I want to see if I can do it."

Jin glanced behind. "Not yet," he said. "My uncle would not like that." Gripping the front of the pole with his left hand, he swung it so that a bag hung on each side of his body. He set off down the wooden sidewalk.

Mackenzie held up his parcel. "How do you know who each package belongs to?" he asked. "Does this say our name in Chinese?"

"No!" Jin laughed. "If you asked my uncle, he might say yes, but that is not true. He writes something about what is being washed or something that will remind him of the customer. Sometimes, if the person has been rude to him he makes a sign with a bad meaning, like big ears or black teeth or stinky dog."

"What does ours mean?"

"I do not know. I cannot read Chinese very well. I think it says a man who tells stories, something like that. My uncle likes your father, so it will be kind. What were you making with your knife?"

"It's for Nellie. Maybe a little doll."

"Why did you not bring your sister with you today?"

"I didn't want to. I would have been stuck with her on the bridge. She'd probably start crying. I don't like having to look after her downtown. Everyone looks at me funny like I'm a girl."

Jin laughed. "But she is so nice. And you do not have to carry her. Just push her pram."

He doesn't know what it's like to take a little girl around with him, Mackenzie thought. It isn't enjoyable. "You wouldn't think it was so wonderful if you had a sister to take care of."

"I do. I have two sisters. The youngest one is the same age as Nellie. I have an older brother, too."

"I didn't know that. Why haven't I ever seen them? Do they live in the back of the laundry with you?"

"No. They are still in Vancouver with my mother. It was not possible for them to come with my father and me. I miss them." Jin stopped. "Do you still want to try to carry this?"

"You bet!"

Jin let the pole slide from his shoulder and the bags dropped to the boardwalk. "Bend your knees," he said.

Mackenzie handed his package to Jin, slipped under the pole, and straightened his legs. "Ow!" he cried. "It pinches." He started walking but after a few yards the pole seemed to spring from his arm. "Whoa! Now what happened?"

"You have to keep your shoulder up." Jin grabbed the pole and hefted it again. "Steady it with your hand. That will help."

At the end of the block, Mackenzie switched the weight to his other arm. By the time they got in sight of the Canadian Northern Station, both his shoulders ached so badly he wanted to drop the bags and drag them on the boardwalk.

"Stop here," Jin said, holding out his hand. "I will take it again."

"Gladly." Mackenzie dropped the bags, noisily let out his breath and rubbed his arms. "There are grooves in here big enough to fit my finger! And that's after only a couple of blocks. I don't know how you can carry it all over town."

Jin heaved the pole onto his shoulder and continued toward the depot. "This is my job," he said.

"Why didn't your mother come with you and your father?" Mackenzie asked.

"My little sister was very sick. The doctor thought

she might have cholera and she was not allowed to travel on the train."

"Nellie was sick once, too, but it was because of bad milk. What's your brother's name?"

"Shen."

A man in faded work clothes approached on the sidewalk. Jin stopped and pressed the bags against a building to make room. Muttering an oath, the man scowled at Jin and spit into the street.

Jin didn't blink. Had he heard? "I don't know why he did that," Mackenzie said. "There was lots of room for you and him to get by."

"For some people," Jin said, "there is never room for me. They don't want me here at all."

That was true, Mackenzie knew. He had seen a gang of little boys taunt Jin. And grown men had sworn at him and pushed him to the ground. It must make you feel miserable to be treated like that. Mackenzie wished he knew how he could help his friend.

"I'm glad you're here," Mackenzie said. "When will the rest of your family come?"

"It is taking a long time for my sister to get better. My mother will send a telegram when they buy their train tickets. I hope that is soon."

"What does your father do at the laundry, Jin? He doesn't come out to the front very often."

"My father gets up early in the morning and builds the fires that heat the water. For many hours he washes clothes. Then he must go to sleep so that he can get up the next day. Sometime my father will have his own laundry. Then I won't have to obey my uncle."

"What does he say?"

"He bosses me all the time. Before I do a delivery he tells me over and over what to do and where to go. When I come back he asks me where I went and tells me I took too long. I am like his slave."

"He's not like that when you're not there. He always tells me how hard you work. He says you are his pride, his jewel."

"Hunh! He doesn't like me enough to let me go to the Exhibition."

"No?"

"He says that many people will come to the city who need their clothes washed. There will be too much work for me to do."

Jin turned onto Twenty-First Street toward the Lucky Star Café.

"Goodbye," Mackenzie called. Then he noticed who was standing in front of the station and went over to investigate.

ALBERT WAS AT THE ROLLER RINK when he said he would be, pacing in the lobby. Spotting Mackenzie, he held up a pair of flashy metal skates.

"Mack!" he said. "Look at these. They're brand new. They're called Knights. My father just bought them for me."

"Let me see one," Mackenzie said. He ran his finger along the shiny footplate and spun each of the four rollers, listening to their soft whir. "I thought you didn't need to have your own skates here," he said.

"You don't. Most people rent them." Albert sat down and set the other skate on the floor. "They strap onto your boot," he said, bending over. "Like this." He put his foot onto the plate and buckled up two leather straps, one around his heel and the other over the top of his boot. "It's that simple."

"What if I slip and hit the floor?" Mackenzie said. "Isn't it made out of concrete?"

"You won't fall."

Mackenzie handed Albert the second skate. He wasn't sure he could believe his friend. He still fell sometimes when he was ice-skating.

"I saw your mother by the station," Mackenzie said.

Tugging on a leather strap, Albert asked, "What was she doing?"

"She had that sign about the Women's Christian Immigration League."

"Oh, that."

"There was a woman there and her children and her husband who looked like Galicians just off the train. They were pretty scared. Your mother was leading them out of the station and pointing at things and talking to them. They didn't look like they understood much."

"Probably not." Albert stood up. "My mother spends hours with those people. She says they have to learn to be like us, and the sooner the better. But I don't think they're going to change."

I shouldn't have said anything, Mackenzie thought. It just makes Albert grumpy. "Nice skates," he said.

Pushing off with one foot, Albert glided away, the rollers purring over the lobby floor. Slowing down, he spun around to face Mackenzie.

"They're fantastic!" he said. "These are the best skates you can buy. Look, Mack." Albert pointed through a pair of large windows set in a wall. "That'll be you."

Boys Mackenzie's age jostled together in small gangs or rushed in single file – with their arms on the hips of the boy in front – along the oval wall that bordered the rink. Groups of two or three women or girls and a few couples skated arm in arm, their legs pushing in unison, left, and right, and left. The few men and some older boys skated on their own. They were moving faster than the girls and women and they swooped in and out and past them with quick gliding steps.

"Are you next?" Startled, Mackenzie turned to find an older boy standing at his side, a pair of roller skates hanging from each hand. Albert was gone. "Sit down," the older boy told Mackenzie, kneeling in front of the bench. He yawned, holding a hand up to cover his mouth, then said, "Put your foot in. Keep it still."

With his open hand the boy hit the front of the footplate until it fit snugly over Mackenzie's boot. He pulled a long-handled screwdriver from his trousers pocket and locked the plate in place.

"The other one."

When the boy moved to the next skater, Mackenzie set the laundry parcel under a seat and pushed himself to his feet. Clutching the backs of benches he wobbled toward the windowed wall and through an open door into the arena. Hundreds of steel rollers ground over the concrete and click-click-clicked like busy insects as they struck the cracks in the floor. The sound of excited voices echoed from the rounded roof of the building.

How do you get going? Mackenzie wondered as a brass band began to play. About a dozen men wearing the red military uniforms of the 105th Regimental Band sat on chairs at the end of the rink. Two drummers stood at their sides, their large bass drum and smaller snare drum set on bamboo tripods. A conductor, dressed in an officer's uniform with gold braid hanging from his shoulders, pumped his arms vigorously to lead the musicians.

As the other skaters sailed past, Mackenzie caught bursts of laughter and snatches of conversations shouted above the music. Everyone else in the arena, it seemed to him, was moving effortlessly.

Like a stiff-legged man walking without his cane, Mackenzie shuffled his feet toward the chest-high wall at the side of the rink. As he closed in on it, an older boy raced alongside him, knocking against his arm and spinning him around. His feet shot out from under him and Mackenzie dropped bottom-first onto the concrete.

Struggling to his knees as other skaters turned sharply to miss him, he crawled back to the wall and teetered onto his feet.

Mackenzie caught sight of Albert with three other boys at the far end of the rink. The four spread themselves out on a pretend starting line then sped away in a race around the oval. Weaving around the slower skaters, Albert quickly took the lead. When he passed Mackenzie he was pumping his arms and taking the long strides of a racer on ice skates.

Suddenly both of Mackenzie's arms were gripped at the elbows and he shot off down the side of the rink, held tightly between two skaters. When he caught his balance and felt his feet rolling steadily beneath him, he glanced to his side.

Eunice McMahon giggled. "You look like a lost puppy," she said. "Don't you know how to do this?"

"He's just learning, aren't you Mackenzie?" Ruth Anne Hardcastle, Mackenzie now knew, was clutching his other elbow. Both girls were in his class at Victoria School. This wasn't the only time they'd shown up at the same place as him and Albert.

"You can't just stand around," Eunice said, "or you'll get yourself hurt."

"Let me go." The last thing I want, Mackenzie thought, is to have people see me with these two.

"Not until you learn to do this properly," Eunice said. "Don't worry. I know what I'm doing. This is how I taught my little brother."

"I'm not your little brother." Mackenzie tried to pull free from the girls' tight grip but stopped when one skate shot out from under him.

Albert sprinted past, followed closely by the three boys.

"Lift your feet," Ruth Anne said, nudging up her glasses. "Left, right, left. Do it in time with us."

Mackenzie hadn't moved his feet off the concrete since the girls had grabbed him. He raised his left foot, wobbled on his right leg, and quickly set his foot back down.

"Try again," Ruth Anne said. "You'll get it."

They had come to the end of the rink. Mackenzie felt himself being swept around the corner and back toward the other end of the arena. "I'll do it by myself. Now let me go!" Pulling his arm to try and break free, he remembered Albert's nickname for Eunice. "Badger Breath," he muttered.

Immediately Eunice's fingers stabbed like railway spikes into his arm.

"Don't ever call me that," she said. Then, "Faster, Ruth Anne."

"What are you doing?" Mackenzie tugged his arms but the girls held on tightly.

"Do you see that wall at the end of the arena?" Eunice asked. "If you don't apologize, Mackenzie, you're going to be splattered into it like a bug on my father's motor car." Eunice was silent for a few seconds, then, "On three, Ruth Anne."

Mackenzie watched the wall racing toward him.

"Eunice," Ruth Anne said, "don't. He could get really hurt."

"Take it back, Mackenzie."

They were a few yards from the wall and not slowing down.

"One. Two –"

"All right! I'm sorry." The girls steered away, taking their captive with them. Once around the corner, they let go and skated off. Mackenzie began to slow down. He held his arms out in front of him until he struck the side wall. Too embarrassed to stay on the rink, he began to pull himself hand-over-hand toward the door to the lobby.

Albert stopped at his side. "What were you doing with those two? You looked like a girl skating with them."

"I wasn't *with* them. They grabbed me and I couldn't get away. I don't know how to skate, remember?" And they wouldn't have come close, Mackenzie told himself, if you'd stuck around.

"Sorry. I was racing and I had to finish. I beat all three of them. I'll teach you now, show you everything you need to know."

"How did you get to be so good?"

"My father taught me. We used to go skating all the time when we lived in Minneapolis, Minnesota. It's great once you get on to it."

"Not today," Mackenzie said. "I've had enough." And I'm not sticking around where those girls are, he thought, drawing himself further along the wall.

"Don't let them scare you. I'll get you skating as well as anybody."

"Nope."

"Well, stay and watch me. Those boys want to race again. This time for money."

"Where are they from?"

"Princess School. I know I can beat them. I wasn't even trying before."

Mackenzie pulled himself through the door to the lobby and rolled up to a bench. "Good luck. I'll come as soon as I get these darn things off."

Mackenzie didn't look back into the arena until, returning the skates to a counter, he heard a woman scream. With everyone else in the lobby, he dashed to one of the windows.

The band had stopped playing. The skaters were silent and still, many of them gathered around someone lying on the concrete floor. Quickly Mackenzie scanned the rink. There was no sign of Albert but the three boys he'd been racing stood by themselves, peering toward the injured skater. His heart lurched as Mackenzie realized who was on the floor. Pushing through the onlookers blocking the door, he dashed across the arena.

"He came out of nowhere," Mackenzie heard a woman say as he forced his way into the crowd. She spoke quickly in a high voice. "Mrs. Whitney and I were skating together and this mob of youngsters raced past on either side of us. That one caught his foot on her skate. These children care little for anyone but themselves. Their racing should not be allowed in a public arena."

There were two people on the floor, Mackenzie saw. A woman sat with her feet splayed in front of her and a dazed look on her face. Her friend, the one talking, knelt behind her supporting the woman's shoulders.

Three feet away, Albert lay on his back with his arms draped over his stomach. His left arm looked like the branch of a tree that someone had snapped but had not been able to cleanly break into two. The splintered end of a bone had pierced the skin above his wrist.

A man was on his knees, leaning over so that his face was close to Albert's and talking in a quiet voice. When Mackenzie knelt on his friend's other side, Albert smiled weakly. Already the colour was draining from his cheeks.

"I was winning, Mack," Albert said. "There was just one more lap to go. And then some old cow swerved right in front of me." He nodded at the man caring for him. "He says I broke my arm. But he won't let me see it. Blasted luck. What's it look like?"

Mackenzie shot another glance at the fracture. Feeling his stomach turn, he looked quickly away. "Does it hurt?" he asked.

"No. I can't feel a thing."

"You should be glad of that, young fellow," the man beside them said. "It'll hurt like the dickens when the shock wears off."

"Get him off the floor," another man said, leaning over Mackenzie. "See if he can walk. My motor car is parked in front of the arena. I'll drive him to the hospital."

Someone took Mackenzie's shoulders from behind and pulled him back.

"I'll go to the ABC," Mackenzie said, straightening up. "I'll tell your father."

"Thanks, Mack."

Mackenzie saw Albert press his lips together like you do when you're trying to stop yourself from crying. Then he lost sight of his friend as two men wrapped their arms around Albert and lifted him gingerly to his feet.

WHEELING HIS CHAIR away from his desk at *The Daily Phoenix* newspaper, Mackenzie's father slipped a pencil behind his ear. Nearby, visible through the open door of the editor's office, Mr. Aikin read from a loose pile of papers spread on his desk.

"That's terrible about Albert," Mackenzie's father said. "Just terrible. It'll certainly slow him down for awhile. It must've been a shock for you to see his arm like that." He reached up and lay his hand on Mackenzie's shoulder. "Good for you to think about telling Mr. Crawley. That's using your noggin." He checked the clock on the wall then leaned back and stretched his arms over his head.

"We're running late again," he said. "It's always like this before the Fair. There'll be thousands more people in town this week and we have all kinds of stories to get ready for them. And advertisements! Every merchant wants a share of the visitors' purses. It's a wonder we get anything printed at all."

"Mother asked me to remind you to buy some things that she needs," Mackenzie said, turning the roller on his father's typewriter to move a sheet of yellow paper one way – chunk, chunk, chunk, chunk – and then back.

"I promised her I would," Mackenzie's father said, sitting forward in his chair, "but I haven't been able to leave yet." He pulled the pencil from behind his ear and tapped the sharpened tip against his fingernail. "Keep yourself busy for a few shakes," he said. "I won't be much longer. Then we'll walk home together for supper. I'll be coming back and working late tonight." Tossing the pencil onto his desk, Mackenzie's father turned in his chair and began to type.

Mackenzie set the laundry on the edge of his father's desk, walked over to the counter that ran across the front of the room and ducked through an opening. Picking up a copy of *The Daily Phoenix*, he sidled toward Miss Price. The clerk's wrought-iron cage, which sat on one end of the counter, had a small opening in the front like the wicket of a bank teller.

A woman stood facing Miss Price, her head bowed as she searched through the purse she'd set on the counter. She wore a light blue dress with a high collar and buttons that ran from her chin to her toes. A black veil with a fine mesh and large black dots hung from the woman's hat and hid her face. Mackenzie couldn't see the hat clearly through the veil but its two long blue feathers pierced the mesh at the back of her head. A dark blue feather boa looped around her neck, ran down her arms and trailed below her hands.

"Madame wishes to make a notice," the woman said as she unfolded a piece of paper she'd taken from her purse.

Miss Price picked up her pen and held it poised above a sheet of yellow paper.

What sort of advertisement does she have? Mackenzie wondered, trying to catch a glimpse of the woman's paper. Is she from the Fair?

"*Scientific Palmistry*," the woman read slowly. "*Madame La Claire inform the public of her wonderful power in reading the history of his life by looking –*"

"Wait, please." Miss Price held up her left hand. When she had finished writing, she added, "You have to stop so that I can catch up. I don't want to miss anything." She smiled. "I think that you mean powers, not power. Informs, not inform. Their lives, not his life."

"Yes."

"Start again," Miss Price said, "after, 'reading the history.'"

The woman slid the tip of her index finger along the lines of her handwriting. *The history of his life,*" she said, "*by looking at the palm of his hand.*" She stopped abruptly when Miss Price's hand shot up.

The fortune teller's having trouble with English, Mackenzie thought. What language does she really speak? There were so many people in the city who talked with accents it was hard to tell where they all came from.

He looked toward Mr. Aikin's office. The stub of the editor's cigar slumped into his glass ashtray as he measured the length of a story with a two-foot wooden ruler. He scribbled numbers onto a separate piece of paper and rubbed the top of his balding head.

"Just give me what you have written," Mackenzie heard Miss Price say. "I'll correct things as I go along. That will be easier for both of us."

"Yes."

"Now," Miss Price said, reading slowly as she wrote, "...*the palm of the hand telling the Past, Present, and Future. Her Readings are given to ladies and gentlemen and advice is offered on all matters of business or domestic affairs. Her charges are reasonable. She tells you the name of your future companion, what planet you were born under and what part of the country is the luckiest for you. She will be at home at 909 Main Street for all visitors during Fair week.*" Miss Price paused. "You have regular hours, don't you? You should say when you are available."

"Yes."

Mackenzie smiled. His mother said fortune tellers made up whatever they thought people wanted to hear.

Miss Price seemed to know this one. Was she foolish enough to believe what the woman claimed?

MACKENZIE'S FATHER rested his arm on the side of Henry Lavallée's dray while the teamster waited in line to cross the Traffic Bridge. The wagonload of thick planks smelled of freshly sawed lumber.

"Are these for the Exhibition?" Mackenzie's father asked.

"Yes, this is our third trip today," Henry Lavallée said, scratching under his blue beret. A powerful man, with a chest as round as the wooden barrels he sometimes carried, Henry Lavallée was said to have arms as hard as oak boards. "The men are still building the grandstand. It keeps getting bigger and bigger. There will be thousands of people wanting a seat on the bleachers. Even this load will not be enough to finish it."

Mackenzie walked past the glistening green wagon that shone each day like it had been painted that very morning. His friend Stanley stood in front of the team, loosely gripping the bridle of one of the horses. Stanislav Murawsky was a few years older than Mackenzie and this summer he had become Henry Lavallée's helper.

"Hi, Stanley," Mackenzie said, patting the granite-hard forehead of each Clydesdale in turn. Snorting, Blackie swung his big head into Mackenzie's chest. His partner, Star, stretched his neck and fluttered his lips as if he wanted to whisper in Mackenzie's ear. "Are you taking more loads to the Exhibition tomorrow?"

"Every day we will go to the Fair. Mr. Lavallée says we will be busy from morning until dark."

"You won't have time to see much."

"No. But I will make double my usual wages. And that will make my mother very happy."

With a jangle of chains, the wagon in front of the boys staggered forward a yard then stopped. Stanley looked further up the line.

"We will be moving soon," he said, tightening his hold on the bridle. "I saw your Birdman in his aeroplane," he added. "Those wings made of cloth and everything held together with little sticks and wires. I think that a good wind will blow it all apart."

"No," Mackenzie said. "He's flown it hundreds of times. It might look flimsy but it can carry that big motor and Mr. Martin."

"But not me. I want a solid wagon, like Mr. Lavallée's."

"Okay." Mackenzie smiled. "Not you, Stanley." Still, he thought, that aeroplane is lots strong enough for me.

TWENTY MINUTES LATER, Mackenzie and his father walked along the side of their house and into the backyard. Squatting in a wallow of dry dirt near the bottom of the steps, his sister Nellie spotted them and called to be picked up. A moment later the back door opened and Mackenzie's mother stepped onto the stoop and over a dozen large carrots spotted in dirt and with their wilting stems still attached.

"Mother!" Mackenzie cried, "you won't guess what happened to Albert!"

"What's that boy done now?" Mackenzie's mother frowned at Nellie. "Ted," she said, "I don't know what to do with our daughter. Look at her! You'd think she hadn't been washed in a week. I swear it's been only five minutes."

"Mother. He was roller skating and he fell and –"

"That will have to wait, Mackenzie. Supper is well past being ready. I need you to run these carrots over to Mr. Arnold. He's given us more of his new potatoes. That and onions is about all he has growing. I'm sure he'll like something different." Mackenzie dropped the laundry package on the steps and picked up the carrots.

"Take Nellie along," his mother said. "She always likes to see Rose."

When he got to the back alley, Mackenzie could smell the mix of wagon grease, warm manure and the dusty, dry stalks of last year's hay that drifted from the open door of Mr. Arnold's stable. Their neighbour was watering his horse, whose long lead was tied to a stake beside his house.

"My mother asked me to give you these," Mackenzie said.

"Thank you, Mack," Mr. Arnold said, taking the carrots by their stems.

Rose swung her head up from the water trough, curled her upper lip over her teeth and nickered softly.

"She's a smart old gal," Mr. Arnold said, holding out a carrot to Nellie. "Would you like to feed her one? She loves her carrots."

Nellie turned to stare into the horse's eyes. Then, pressing her back into Mackenzie's shoulder, she held out her hand. Rose bit the carrot from its stem, chewed once, and swallowed. Nellie giggled.

"Good girl." Mr. Arnold handed Nellie another carrot and asked Mackenzie, "Are you going to the Exhibition Hall at the Fair tomorrow?"

"Yes, with my father."

"You'll have to watch for my pie. I have one entered in the competition again. Rhubarb. This might be the year I get a ribbon, do you think?"

"I hope so. Your pies are delicious."

Mackenzie stepped back. "We have to go, Nellie," he said. "By the time we get you washed up, Mother will have the food on the table."

"Tell your mother to let me know when she needs more spuds, Mack," Mr. Arnold said. "And don't forget, you're welcome to take Rose for a ride whenever you like."

"Thank you."

On the way back to their house, Mackenzie walked past the concrete box closet that sat at the rear of their lot. Until two weeks ago, the closet had held night soil taken every morning from their chamber pots and picked up once a week in a reeking rig called a honey wagon. Now water and sewer pipes connected their house to the lines that ran under the street.

Mackenzie bent down, scooped up a stone from the alley and threw it at the box closet. The rock cracked off the side a few inches from where a row of flies clung to the warm concrete. One after another, the flies lazily rose into the air then dropped back onto the box. Thankful he had nothing more to do with the closet, Mackenzie swung his sister onto his back and hurried into the house for supper.

The Daily Phoenix

MONDAY, AUGUST 5, 1912

DARING MIDNIGHT ROBBERY ON ALBERT AVENUE

Bills and Silver Taken

The residence of J. Lozar on Albert Avenue was burglarized this past Saturday evening. Thieves boldly entered a tent in the backyard in which Mr. and Mrs. Lozar and two children were sleeping in order to escape the stifling heat of their house, resulting from the near-record temperatures of recent days. Mr. Lozar's wearables were gone through and about $50 in cash taken, as well as a pair of men's shoes. The midnight marauders then forced an entrance into the house and stole a collection of silverware, including a mono-grammed serving platter recently arrived from Mrs. Lozar's family in England.

A cohort of constables under the able direction of Sergeant Devereux spent Sunday morning combing the yards of Mr. Lozar and his neighbours for possible clues. One sharp-eyed officer spotted Mr. Lozar's shoes behind some bushes no more than 100 feet from the scene. The thief obviously had checked the fit of the shoes and decided that while the newly pol-ished oxfords gleamed nicely in the moonlight, they were not of a size to be of any use to him.

Sergeant Devereux told *The Daily Phoenix* that this robbery may be connected to other recent burglaries but he is tight-lipped about the results of his investi-gation thus far.

CHAPTER TWO
Tuesday, August 6, 1912

S QUEEZING THE PENNIES HIS MOTHER HAD GIVEN
him to buy a present for Albert, Mackenzie cut
across Broadway Avenue, easily avoiding the few
motor cars and wagons on the wide street. At the end
of the block he slowed and entered the fragrant air of
Allwood Harness and Confectionery. The small shop
smacked of well-oiled leather, bitter dyes, unwrapped
chocolates and sugary-sweet candies.

Along one inside wall, long loops of reins and
traces, sets of harnesses and horse hobbles, steel
buckles, braided bellybands, cowbells and horsewhips
hung from brass hooks. Suspended from the metal
ceiling were stacks of horse collars and sweat pads. On
the other side of the room glass-fronted cabinets ran
from the front of the shop to the back. Paper-lined
glass shelves displayed candies, chocolates, fudges and
toffees of every size and colour, some heaped in

mounds on a saucer, some sitting alone in a gilt-lined box like a royal gift and others wrapped in coloured tissue stamped with the name of their maker in some far-off European country.

Mackenzie gazed hungrily at the confections. Behind the counter two women wearing white gloves and white aprons over their long-sleeved dresses worked at a table. One of the clerks turned, brushed her hands over the front of her apron and smiled at Mackenzie.

"Hello, Miss Avery."

"Hello, young man. What would you like this morning?"

"Mmm." Mackenzie's eyes were drawn to a tray of chocolate-covered nuts near the woman's elbow. He shifted sideways and peered through the glass at the coloured balls of rock-hard candy. "I have only three cents."

Miss Avery reached down and slipped a square of white paper from a stack on the table. Laying the sheet on the steel tray of a balance that sat on top of the cabinet, she said, "Well, let's see what we can do."

Soon the paper was spread open in Mackenzie's hand. Without thinking he chose a round orange candy and popped it in his mouth. Sour! he thought, screwing up his face. I'd better save these, they're Albert's favourites. Closing his hand around the paper, he walked across the store and stopped at a reddish brown sidesaddle decorated with fancy stitching.

"Are you gawking or buying?" a man's voice called out.

Mackenzie turned toward two men who stood near a workbench at the back of the harness shop. The owner of the store had a shiny leather apron tied at his waist. In one hand he held a long strap that hung over the side of the bench and in the other a wooden-handled awl. The dark-skinned man beside him wore a stetson cowboy hat with a single feather stuck in the band. Behind him, leaning against the back wall of the shop, a boy about Mackenzie's age stared out from under the peak of a grey tweed cap. Cupped in the boy's hand was a square of white paper.

"I'm just looking," Mackenzie answered, then leaned close to admire the elaborately stamped finish on a pure black saddle with sheepskin wool lining.

"I figured," the owner said. "You go right ahead." Then to his customer he added, "You wouldn't really mistake him for a seasoned cowpuncher, would you?"

The dark-skinned man chuckled.

"Mind you don't touch anything with sticky fingers," the owner added before looking back to the workbench.

"We're buying this one," the boy said, joining Mackenzie on the other side of the saddle.

"For you?"

"My brother," the boy said. Rubbing his hand on his trousers, he grabbed the horn and straightened the saddle on its stand. "He's got a job as a ranch hand."

"Does he have his own horse?"

"Yep."

"Do you?"

"My father lets me use one of his. When I'm older, he'll give me my own."

"Junior!" the man called. "Come and take these to the buggy. Leave the saddle. We're not getting it today."

The boy released his grip and walked to the back of the shop. As he and his father gathered up their gear, the owner asked, "Does that 101 Ranch outfit pay well, Joseph?"

"As good as you get hauling hay or stooking wheat," the other man said, then laughed. "And it's a heck of a lot easier. Food's good, too." He lifted his hat and wiped his hand over his forehead. "They're real sticklers about your gear, though. You get inspected. Everything has to be top-notch."

They're talking about the Wild West Show, Mackenzie thought. The 101 Ranch from Oklahoma is here for the Fair. What would that Indian man be doing working for them? Mackenzie opened his hand and gazed at the candies. One more, he told himself.

A few minutes later, the paper once more closed around the sticky sweets, Mackenzie strolled past Victoria School. The building boasted three-storey yellow brick towers, tall skinny windows framed in stone and an arched main entrance cut deep into the front wall. During the long, hot month of June,

Mackenzie's gaze had often wandered from the black-board, out a second-floor window and across Broadway Avenue to a construction site.

The Farnam Block had risen quickly and now a skeleton of wooden scaffolding clung to the almost finished structure. Men in loose-fitting overalls and long-sleeved shirts sauntered along the walkways of thick planks laced to skinny poles. Some hauled red bricks to add to the piles spaced along the planks. Others used a winch to bring up buckets of soupy mortar that had been mixed in troughs on the ground below. Bricklayers slapped the mortar onto their latest row, then set down another line of bricks and tapped them in place with the handles of their trowels. By the time school started again in September, the scaffolding would be gone and the building filled. Albert's father, Mackenzie knew, had already signed up people to take most of the suites and shops. The city was growing so fast, Mr. Crawley said, it seemed like there were never going to be enough places for people to live.

Crossing the intersection at the end of the school grounds, Mackenzie followed the trail of newly planted trees down Broadway Avenue North to Albert's home. He had a few minutes to see how his friend was doing, then he had to meet his mother and Nellie downtown.

ALBERT'S HOUSE sat in the midst of a row of empty lots near the high eastern bank of the river. From the back steps, it was possible to see over the tops of the riverbank trees and across the water to the bustling streets of downtown.

Mackenzie found his friend sitting in the screened front porch, a creamy white cast resting on the wide wooden arm of his chair.

"Come on in!" Albert said.

"How's your arm?" Mackenzie asked, settling into a chair. He reached out and rapped his knuckles on the cast. "Can you feel that?"

"No. But the doc says I can't leave the house until he gives the word. I'm stuck here until he comes back tomorrow morning."

"You're going to miss the Exhibition."

"I know. But there are still three more days after today. Who are you going with?"

"My father. We're taking the train out this afternoon." Mackenzie set the candies on the arm of Albert's chair and unfolded the paper. "These are for you."

"Thanks, Mack." Albert set a chocolate on his tongue and closed his mouth.

"Is your mother upset about you getting hurt?"

Albert chewed on the sweet. "She was," he said. "Except, we got robbed and now that's all she can talk about."

"Robbed! When did that happen?"

"Last night. My parents came to pick me up at the hospital. By then my cast was hard enough for me to leave. When we got back, my mother knew as soon as she was through the door that things had been stolen. She usually keeps her jewellery in the safe in my father's office. But he'd brought it home on Friday because she'd invited some ladies over to see her things. It was all gone. Rings, brooches, necklaces. Even some cufflinks and my father's watch that he'd left on his dresser. My father exploded. He kicked everything in sight except the cat! He'd just had his shoes polished but by the time he'd calmed down, they looked like they'd been through a threshing machine."

"Did the police come?" Mackenzie asked. "What did they do?"

"Searched all over the place, inside and out. Didn't find anything. But I heard two of the coppers talking. They think it's a gang doing all these robberies. They have an idea who it might be."

"Who?"

"They figure there's someone who's seen what's inside the houses that are robbed." Albert stopped and looked at Mackenzie. "Get it? Someone who's been there."

Mackenzie didn't get it. How was he supposed to know who had been inside Albert's house? "I don't follow," he said.

"Think about that Chinaman friend of yours. He and other guys who work for Chinese laundries deliver clothes right into people's houses. They get a good look at whatever might be valuable. Then they can tell other Chinamen what they saw and later someone sneaks into the house and takes the stuff."

"Albert, that's ridiculous! So you think that every time someone gets robbed it's because there was a delivery from a Chinese laundry? Who took clothes to your house?"

"You know his name better than I do."

"I don't believe that. Jin wouldn't do it. He's as honest as you or me. And so's his uncle." Mackenzie was getting fed up with Chinese people being blamed for things. "Just because people are different," he said, "doesn't mean –"

"I'm just saying what I heard, Mack. Don't get angry at me." Albert shrugged. "You have to admit, it makes sense."

"No it doesn't. Not if you know what someone's like."

Albert chose another candy. "Anyway, the worst part is that my mother says that was the last straw. She's tired of living in a frontier town. She wants to move back to Minneapolis, Minnesota."

Mackenzie studied his friend, wondering if what Albert was saying was the truth. He reached over and plucked a sweet from the paper wrapping.

"My father says we might," Albert said. "He's working on this big deal to sell a huge block of Saskatoon land. There's someone in Chicago who wants to buy it. They just have to work out the details. He'll find out any day now. If it sells, he'll make a pile of money and we'll be gone."

"You don't want to move, do you?" Mackenzie asked.

"No. This place is a whole lot better than Minneapolis, Minnesota, I can tell you that. Everything's old down there." Albert scowled out the screen window. Then he turned to Mackenzie. "Have you heard about the fly contest?" he asked.

"What's that?"

"Doc McKay started a contest, with prizes. He hates flies and he's going to give money to whoever brings him the most dead ones. My mother and some other women from her church are helping him. It's so people don't get sick so often."

"How much is the prize?"

"Ten dollars for whoever catches the most flies by Saturday. It'll be more the week after."

"That's a lot of money."

"I've got a plan."

Mackenzie wasn't surprised. He eyed the shrinking pile of candies. He'd better leave the rest. "What is it?" he asked. Albert was always dreaming up schemes to make money.

"We can go partners. We split everything fifty-fifty."

"How are we going to get more flies than anybody else?"

"Simple. We don't just wait around and catch the ones we find. We breed them. Do you know how many offspring they produce? We could end up with millions of the little beggars."

Millions? That didn't sound very simple. "Albert, not so fast," Mackenzie said. "Where are you going to keep these flies?"

"Easy. What's the favourite place for them to lay their eggs?"

Mackenzie thought for a moment. "In garbage, I guess. Or manure."

"Correct. So, first, we find some manure. It will have flies buzzing around it and some eggs already laid in it. We take a few flies and some of the manure and seal them up in a container. And then we wait."

Manure, Mackenzie thought. That's going to get awfully stinky, very fast. "Where do you think you're going to store it?"

"I've had lots of time to think about that," Albert said. "I'll tell you what we're going to do."

Mackenzie listened. It didn't take long for him to figure out where he would fit into Albert's plan.

MACKENZIE PUSHED his sister's perambulator along Twenty-First Street toward the Lucky Star Café, located one half block from the Canadian Northern Railway Station. Many of the restaurant's customers were travellers who wanted to enjoy a meal on solid ground. Other clients who lived in the city visited the Lucky Star to buy special foods.

Mackenzie parked Nellie's carriage in front of a window alive with pots of leafy plants. Further back were pyramids made with small green tins and glass bottles of cooking oil. Two kinds of apples were heaped in wooden baskets and bunches of green bananas hung from wooden poles that rose to the ceiling.

Inside the wicker pram, Nellie sat facing Mackenzie, her cheeks slathered with a shiny goo and the fingers of one hand planted inside her mouth.

"You're a mess," Mackenzie said. "You can't go in looking like that." He knelt down and took a damp cloth from a bag resting on the bottom shelf of the carriage. He had taken Nellie to the Hub Café and Confectionery for ice cream so that his mother could enjoy a cup of tea with a friend, Mrs. Armsbitter. Now, if his mother was ready, she would take Nellie and Mackenzie could go to the Fair with his father. Nellie squirmed and cried out, but Mackenzie firmly cupped one hand behind her head and with the other wiped her face. "Okay. I'm done."

Picking up his sister, Mackenzie walked past a Chinese clerk standing in the open doorway. Under a calf-length blue apron the man wore a black bow tie, black suspenders and a striped shirt with a high white collar and sleeves rolled to his elbows. Mackenzie studied the glass counters that surrounded him. In one sat blocks of yellow and white and red-skinned cheeses. Another held slabs of chocolate. Shelf after shelf was filled with trays and baskets of almonds and grapes, oranges, prunes, strawberries and pineapples, jars of pickles and bottles of soft drinks. Another counter held a display of ceramic soup bowls and spoons and boxes of fancy and plain wooden chopsticks. One time when he'd come to the Lucky Star Café with his mother, he'd seen two old Chinese men eating their meal with chopsticks. Is that what Jin uses to eat? he wondered. What would that be like?

Mackenzie parted the bamboo curtain hanging across the door to the restaurant area behind the store and found his mother partly hidden by the tall back of a wooden booth. Giggling, Nellie held out her arms. "Hello, Mother," he said, handing over his sister. "Hello, Mrs. Armsbitter."

His mother's friend was dressed in black – hat, skirt, long-sleeved blouse and gloves – in mourning. Two months earlier, in a spell of hot June weather, Mrs. Armsbitter's baby son had died of typhoid fever. Whenever he saw her, Mackenzie remembered Philip's wake at the Armsbitters' house and the little boy lying so sad and still in his coffin.

"Will there be anything else for you ladies?" a waitress asked, stopping at the booth. The woman's blonde hair was pulled into a bun at the back of her head. She smiled at Nellie as she waited for an answer.

Mackenzie saw Mrs. Armsbitter pinch her lips together and closely examine her cup of tea.

"No, thank you," his mother said. "We'll take our bill now." Nellie picked up a spoon and tap-tap-tapped it onto the table.

"I've got one her size who loves to make music, too," the waitress said. "Thinks my cooking pot is her drum." She walked toward the back of the café, past a couple of empty booths, and stopped at a family with six children crowded in beside the mother and father.

Mrs. Armsbitter glanced at the waitress, leaned across the table, and whispered, "Our new law can't come any too soon." She sniffed and sat up straight against the back of the booth.

"What new law is that?" Mackenzie wondered. He turned to his mother.

Taking the spoon from Nellie, she quietly said to him, "A few months ago the province made a law that prohibits white women from working for Chinese people. Do you know what prohibit means?"

"They're not allowed."

"That's right. Well, now the government wants the law enforced. So, women like that waitress will lose their jobs."

"It's high time," Mrs. Armsbitter said. "It isn't proper for a Celestial to be the boss of a white woman. It's not natural."

Mackenzie saw the waitress sit down at an empty table at the back of the café. Leafing through the pages of a magazine, her finger looped through the handle of an empty cup, the woman looked happy to him. "She won't be able to work here anymore?" he said.

"Certainly not," Mrs. Armsbitter said. "She can always find another position." She drank the last of her tea and primly set the cup on its saucer.

Mackenzie shifted closer to his mother. "What does it mean when Chinese people are called Celestials?" he asked.

Mackenzie's mother turned to her friend. "Do you know? Celestial means heavenly, Mackenzie. I think it's because in ancient times the first Chinese emperors were thought to be like gods who lived in a kind of heaven. When we use it nowadays, I suppose it's like we're making fun of them. I hadn't thought about that before."

Nellie reached for an empty cup. When her mother moved it further into the middle of the table, she whimpered.

"I think your sister needs a nap, Mackenzie," his mother said. "And we still have tea left in our pot. Take her back outside, please, and get her settled into her pram. In fact, you have time to push her around the block once. That might put her to sleep."

"I'm supposed to meet Father," Mackenzie said. "We're going to the Fair."

"Don't worry about him. He's so busy this week he won't even notice you're late. Away you go!"

Mackenzie heaved his sister onto his shoulder and trudged to the front of the building. I shouldn't have to do this, he told himself. I'm a boy. But his mood changed as soon as he walked out the door. There, coming toward him along the sidewalk was someone who liked picking up his baby sister.

Mackenzie smiled. "Hi, Jin," he said.

Jin set his pole and bags against the side of the building and took Nellie in his arms. He cooed in her ear and tickled her back.

What, Mackenzie wondered, would Mrs. Armsbitter think if she saw a Chinese boy hugging a white baby? Probably that it's not natural.

Jin turned to Mackenzie. "I cannot stop," he said. "My uncle told me I must be back in fifteen minutes. He thinks I can run everywhere I go."

"Where are you taking this laundry?" Mackenzie asked.

"To a house on Third Avenue," Jin said. "It is not heavy this time, only shirts and blouses."

"I'll walk a little with you. Just put Nellie in her pram. She'll be fine."

The two boys set off down the sidewalk, with Nellie babbling to herself and keeping her eyes on Jin.

"My mother just told me that there's a new law," Mackenzie said. "One that says white women can't work for Chinese people. Did you know that?"

"Yes."

"Doesn't that make you angry?"

"My uncle says it does not help us to get angry. If we are kind to other people, then after a while people will be kind back to us."

"I really wish I could help."

"You are helping. You are already nice."

"I guess so." Mackenzie took his hands off the

handle and let the pram roll on its own. "I should turn back so I can give Nellie to Mother again."

"And I will hurry so I am not late for my uncle."

The boys exchanged goodbyes. Mackenzie lifted the front of the pram off the ground and, calling, "Hang on!" spun the carriage around on two wheels. Falling onto her back, Nellie kicked her feet and giggled. Jin is my friend, Mackenzie told himself. But he's different from me, too. Maybe Albert's a little bit right. In some ways Chinese people aren't the same as us.

MACKENZIE'S FATHER glanced at his feet and stood up. "I'm going to make one stop before we catch the train," he said. Mackenzie followed him out of *The Daily Phoenix* office. "I have to get my shoes shined. Have I ever taken you to Brittner's before?"

Mackenzie shook his head.

"Your mother thinks it's a terrible place," his father said, starting down the sidewalk. "But I try to get there for a shine every few weeks."

"Why doesn't she like it?"

"Mr. Brittner, mostly. He's an odd-looking man to begin with and he doesn't waste any time trying to improve things. More than anything, he looks like he's still living in the Wild West. His clothes don't see the laundry too often and his moustache probably hasn't been trimmed in twenty years." Mackenzie's father chuckled. "He's a decent enough chap, but you have to wonder how he can keep a business going without scaring off his customers."

"He shines shoes?"

"Not himself. He always has one or two boys around to do that. And he runs a kind of a general store, too. Most of his merchandise is second-hand and not very good quality. Mr. Brittner likes to buy his supplies at the lowest possible price. Say a merchant in North Battleford closes his doors. Mr. Brittner might offer a few dollars for his goods. Or a man dies. Or if a homesteader runs out of money and abandons his stake, Mr. Brittner will pay a little to take the man's kit off his hands. That means that almost everything he sells is cheaper than you'd pay somewhere else."

"Mother doesn't like that?"

"She went there once when we first moved here and she needed a few things we didn't bring from Winnipeg. From the way she described it, you'd think she'd stepped into the house of the devil. Besides Mr. Brittner, she saw shifty-looking shoeshines, clouds of cigar smoke and dusty piles of other people's castaways! She doesn't like it that I go there once in awhile. And she certainly would get after us if she knew you'd tagged along with me."

Mackenzie's father turned to his son and kept his gaze on him until Mackenzie looked up. "Mr. Brittner is harmless," he said. "Completely harmless. I know his heart's in the right place and I'm sure this visit won't hurt you in any way. But it has to be just between you and me."

Mackenzie felt a smile break over his face. He liked doing things with his father. If it had to be kept a secret from his mother, that only made the adventure more special.

"Why do you get your shoes shined there?" he asked.

"It's part of my beat. As a reporter, I have to keep in touch with what men are thinking about and what they're saying to each other. The best places for me to hear gossip are the barbershop and the shoeshine. I go to different ones every week. It just happens to be Mr. Brittner's turn today."

A few blocks north of *The Daily Phoenix* office, not far from the Canadian Pacific Railway yards, Mackenzie's father stopped before a hand-printed sign in a dusty window. "Shoeshines on Premises," it read.

"Here we are."

Mackenzie looked past his father. Above an open doorway a larger sign announced, "Brittner's General Store and Used Goods Emporium." The inside of the building looked grey and gloomy. I wonder what I'll find in there? Mackenzie wondered. I'd never go in this place by myself.

"Get your shine here, Mr. Davis!" a voice called as they entered. Mackenzie saw a stocky man rise from one of two wooden armchairs that stood on a waist-high platform. An apron stained by smears of dark brown and black polish hung from the man's neck. The wooden handles of a half-dozen brushes poked from a row of pockets sewn across the bottom of the apron. Pulling a cloth from one of the pockets, the man sprang to the floor. "No waiting today, Mr. Davis," he said. "Step right up."

"Righto, Bauer," Mackenzie's father said.

A customer sitting in the other chair looked out from behind his copy of *The Daily Phoenix*. After nodding to Mackenzie's father he turned to smile at Mackenzie.

"Oh, hello –" Mackenzie began. He had to stop. The man worked in Harry Tupling's Men's Furnishings. Because he was tall and skinny with a pointed Adam's apple, Mackenzie thought of him as Ichabod Crane, the schoolteacher in the story, *The Legend of Sleepy Hollow*. He didn't know his real name.

"Mr. Warnick," Mackenzie's father said. "How's business?"

"It's a fright," the clerk replied. "Busy as the dickens with the Fair starting. I had to leave Mr. Tupling alone for a short while so I could rush over here and make myself more presentable." He dropped the newspaper onto his lap. "Just about finished, Fletcher?" he asked the shoeshine tugging a cloth briskly back and forth over the toes of his shoes. Skinny and not much taller than Mackenzie, the second shoeshine released his grip from one hand every few seconds to noisily crack his cloth.

"Look around," Mackenzie's father said, nodding toward the back of the store. "There's plenty to see." Stepping onto a stool, he hoisted himself up.

"What's news today, Mr. Davis?" the shoeshine asked.

"The Exhibition, just like Mr. Warnick said. That's all anyone in Saskatoon wants to talk about. What do you boys know that's different?"

Mackenzie stopped listening and turned into the store. Immediately he was drawn to a long cabinet. The shelves inside held men's and ladies' watches, tarnished silver cutlery, stacked china bowls, a bone-handled teapot, and a collection of knives and handguns. Behind the counter sat a cash register. Mackenzie wandered further into the store, to a maze of tables and counters heaped with jumbles of pots and pans, chipped plates, cups and bowls, tools of all sorts and the tangled leather straps, steel loops and buckles of horses' harnesses. Ropes that once might have been lariats and horses' leads lay discarded in a tangled heap in a corner on the floor. A dozen or more men's suit coats and black trousers hung from hooks along one wall. Mackenzie wondered if the previous owners were still alive. He flipped through one of the books he found stacked on a dusty shelf.

A meaty man wearing a soiled, long-sleeved white shirt and black suspenders walked toward Mackenzie from the back of the store. Three or four walnut-sized bumps bulged from the top of his bald head and a shaggy moustache hung over the unlit cigar in his mouth. Mackenzie could see why his mother didn't like this creepy-looking man. He'd feel the same way if his father hadn't just told him Mr. Brittner was harmless.

While turning the pages of the book, Mackenzie watched the man walk behind the counter and heave himself onto a long-legged stool with wooden armrests and a cushioned seat. Pulling a lever to open the cash register, the man dropped coins into the drawer. He spun on the seat to face the shoeshines.

"Hello, Ted!" the man said. "Is that your boy back there? It's high time you brought him in. We'll have to give him a shine. Fletcher! When you're finished with Mr. Warnick, give the Davis boy our young lad's special."

"That's not necessary, Mr. Brittner," Mackenzie's father said. "The boots he has on are hardly worth the polish. I'll bring him back sometime when he's wearing his Sunday shoes."

"Whatever suits you," Mr. Brittner said, taking the cigar from his mouth, hawking up phlegm and sending a brown gob toward a spittoon at the end of the counter. "He'll be welcome here whenever he shows up."

Mackenzie's father stepped down from the chair. He set a coin on his thumbnail and flicked the silver piece high above his head toward the shoeshine. "Well done, Bauer," he said.

"Thank you, sir!" The man snatched the coin from the air.

"Time to go, son," Mackenzie's father called. "We've got to catch the 4:40 train."

Reluctantly, Mackenzie set down a small wooden carpenter's plane he'd found that fit snugly into his palm. There's lots more to see, he thought. If I get a chance, I'm going to come here again.

WITH A SUDDEN JERK, the locomotive pulled the coaches away from the Canadian Northern Station. It was the first time Mackenzie had been on a train since his family moved from Winnipeg one year before. Every seat was taken and latecomers stood at each end of the car. Women wearing fancy dresses and long white gloves shared seats with men garbed in work clothes. Parents with three or four children had been given single seats. Further up the coach Mackenzie spotted a boy from his class at school. They waved to each other and smiled. The boy shared his seat with two others, all of them in short pants, clean shirts and caps pushed back on their foreheads. Mackenzie sat beside his father, who leaned across the aisle to speak with a man twirling a brass-headed walking stick like an army officer's baton.

Mackenzie's father settled into the upholstered back of the seat. "That man's a barker on the midway," he said, raising his voice above the hubbub in the coach. "He's with Princess Victoria's show. He spent the afternoon handing out dodgers downtown and he says he can hardly wait to get to his tent and start drawing in the curious."

Mackenzie kept his eye on the man with the walking stick. "In *The Daily Phoenix* it said that Princess Victoria is only twenty-five and a half inches tall and weighs twenty pounds. Is that possible?" he asked.

"I saw that, too. It's hard to believe, isn't it? Of course, they'll say anything to get people to come to their show." Mackenzie's father raised his eyebrows. "We may have to buy two tickets and see for ourselves."

"Sure!"

The clack-clack, clack-clack of the train's double wheels grew lighter as if the coach were lifting off the steel rails. When Mackenzie looked out the window, he saw they were on the bridge. He peered far down to the river.

Four adults and at least a dozen children, the smallest ones carried by a parent, waded in the swift, green water. Fully clothed except for the shoes and boots left on the sandy shore, the men and boys wore colourful baggy shirts and trousers and the women and girls threadbare dresses and large silver crucifixes.

"Galicians," his father said, looking over Mackenzie's shoulder. "There are more arriving every day. They're probably living in tents far from a water tap with no other place to wash. This city's booming, Mack."

Pressing his nose against the glass, Mackenzie watched the bathers splashing in the river until the train was off the bridge and onto the riverbank. Soon they stopped at the temporary depot on the fairgrounds.

Spilling onto the platform with the other passengers, Mackenzie and his father made their way to the entrance gates. While his father was paying for their tickets, Mackenzie heard the locomotive's whistle and watched the train steam backwards on its return trip downtown.

A street as long as two city blocks ran from the gates to the Exhibition buildings. Both sides of the passageway were lined with midway tents, food booths and amusement rides. The whole boisterous alley was packed with fairgoers milling in a dusty, fragrant din. Over the buzz of the thousands of visitors rose the voices of the midway barkers, the rattle and toot of many small but energetic bands and the chug-chug of unseen steam engines that powered a Ferris wheel, a merry-go-round and other rides entertaining hordes of squealing children.

"Stick close to me," Mackenzie's father shouted. "We're off to see the local exhibitions first. We'll find out who won what. If there's time, you can try some rides before I have to get back to the office."

Mackenzie slowed down in front of a canvas tent where a man gripping a ball in his hand stared at three wooden pins set on a table. The man wound up, threw and missed. Seeing his father about to be swallowed by the throng, Mackenzie bolted ahead. Thrilled by the noise and the jostling bodies, Mackenzie wildly cast his eyes from side to side, trying to not miss one thing as he hurried into his father's wake.

The Daily Phoenix

TUESDAY, AUGUST 6, 1912

Grand Prize Competition
Swat the Fly!
Millions of Flies Are To Be Assassinated

The Fly Has Got No Friends and
He Does Not Deserve Any
He Carries Disease to the Baby
And Fills the City Cemetery

The housefly lays its eggs in warm, moist, decaying matter and this can be found in and around even the most cleanly household. The favourite place for its eggs, however, is animal manure and human waste and when it finds these materials it becomes the most dangerous of insects on the western plains. The fly picks up disease organisms and later deposits them on unprotected food.

Catch Flies With a Fly Trap! Smack Flies with a Swatter!
Flies in the Millions Will Be Measured
at the Office of the Medical Health Officer
every Saturday beginning at 8 o'clock a.m.

Grand Prize This Week Will Be $10.00
To the Boy or Girl Who Brings In
the Greatest Number of Flies.
Other Prizes Will Be Awarded.

Swat the Fly!

CHAPTER THREE
Wednesday, August 7, 1912

MACKENZIE FOUND ALBERT SITTING ON THE top step of the stairs leading into a small white building. "ABC Land Sales," read the sign on the wall. "Albert B. Crawley, Sr., Prop."

"How's your arm?" Mackenzie asked.

"Doesn't hurt. What did you see last night?"

"The Ferris wheel was the best. It wasn't even scary. It was getting dark and we were so high we could see the lights from the city. Amazing. Can you go today?"

"Yep. First I have to do some errands for my father. He wired those men in Chicago. They sent a message back. Now I have to take his answer down to the telegraph office. They're going to bite. I know it."

"I hope not," Mackenzie said.

"Me too. Did you get that fly breeder started?"

"Yes, but I don't like it, Albert. I'm going to catch it if my parents see what I've done."

"Quit fussing. You're like an old hen. Why would they look there? No one uses it anymore. You're safe. Help me up, will you?" Albert held out his right arm. When he was on his feet, he took his jackknife from his pocket. "I'll challenge you in splits," he said. "It's about the only thing I can play."

"Here? What if your father sees us?"

"He won't," Albert said, snapping open the blade. "He's busy getting his wire ready." Mackenzie pulled out his knife and followed Albert onto the dirt street. "My mother said she'd take my knife away if she caught me doing this," Mackenzie said, looking over his shoulder as he and Albert lined up three feet apart. "Anyway, aren't you a little off balance with that cast?"

"You go first," Albert said, bringing his feet together. "Don't worry about me."

"It'll cost you money when you lose." Mackenzie wiped the blade of his knife on his trousers, closed his left eye, and aimed.

"It has to stick in the ground," Albert said. "And it can't be more than twelve inches from my foot. That's how we did it in Minneapolis, Minnesota."

"I know how to play splits, Albert." Mackenzie raised his hand and threw the knife. The blade pierced the ground a couple of inches from Albert's shoe.

Albert moved his foot, leaned down to pull the knife from the dirt and handed it to Mackenzie. "Good throw," he said. Slowly Albert wiped the blade of his knife back and forth across the arm of his shirt like a barber sharpening a razor on his strap.

At the end of the block, behind Albert, a crow rested on top of a power pole. Spreading its wings, the bird turned to face the boys and bobbed its head. A second later the sound of its ragged caw reached Mackenzie.

"Are you ready?" Albert asked. Tightening his grip on the ebony handle, he raised the knife shoulder-high, whipped his hand toward the ground, then smiled when the blade stuck almost a foot from Mackenzie's boot.

Mackenzie shifted his foot and quickly made his second throw. Albert followed and soon both boys had their legs spread wide apart.

Opening its wings, the crow lifted into the air and flew to a perch on the peak of a three-storey building. The crow opened its beak. Out of the corner of his eye Mackenzie saw Albert flick his wrist. The bird's raspy voice cawed twice just as Mackenzie felt the knife rip through his boot and tear into his flesh.

"Hey!" An inch of blade had pierced the leather near Mackenzie's little toe. Pulling the knife free, he studied the steel closely.

"Geez. Sorry," Albert said. "Did I get you?"

"What do you think?" Mackenzie said, wiping the blade on the leg of his trousers. "I'm bleeding." Tossing aside Albert's knife, he knelt and undid his laces. He tore off the boot, stuck his finger through the new gash in his sock and then pulled that off, too. "I knew you'd have lousy aim," he said, using the sock to dab at his toe.

"It must have slipped."

Mackenzie poked at the slit in his boot. "My mother's going to see this hole, sure as anything," he said. "She isn't going to like it."

"I can fix that. Let me see it." Albert scooped up a small handful of dirt and spit into his palm a few times to wet it. Then he pressed his hand onto Mackenzie's boot and ground the dirt into the cut. "That's all you have to do," he said. "When it dries you can't even tell."

"What a bunch of guff," Mackenzie said, retying his laces. "Anyway, you lost. You owe me five cents."

Albert fished a coin from his pocket and tossed it toward his friend. As Mackenzie snatched it from the air, the door to the ABC office opened. In a flash, both knives disappeared, Mackenzie's into his pocket and Albert's under his foot. Mr. Crawley was short and round and wore a derby hat low on his forehead. As usual, he was smiling. "Hi, Son," he said. "Mack. Everything's ready, Albert. Come and get my telegram."

CUTTING ACROSS THE STREET a few minutes later, the boys spotted Eunice McMahon and Ruth Anne Hardcastle near the door to McMahon's Dry Goods store. Both girls were bent over at the waist and staring closely at their feet. Eunice had a fly swatter at the ready. Beside her, Ruth Anne held two sides of a man's handkerchief spread apart like a white flag.

Eunice slapped the swatter onto the boardwalk. Immediately Ruth Anne laid the handkerchief down. She pinched the cloth with the tips of her fingers then shook it over a large glass jar.

"They're catching flies!" Albert said. "Come on." When they were closer to the girls, he asked, "What's the matter, Four-Eyes, are you afraid of a little fly?"

"Flies carry diseases," Eunice said, straightening up. "They make people sick. That's why we're killing them. To help people."

Albert chortled. "No you're not. You're killing them so you can go in that contest."

"You think you're going to win a prize?" Mackenzie added. If this is what they were going to do, he and Albert easily could gather more flies than Eunice and Ruth Anne. It would feel great if they won instead of these annoying girls.

"We might," Ruth Anne said.

"How many do you have so far?" Albert peered into the jar. "What's that? Six? Six flies?"

"Ten," Ruth Anne said. "And we've just started."

"You don't stand a chance," Albert said. "Not a chance."

"How many do you have?"

"It doesn't matter how many we have now," Albert said. "The deadline's not until Saturday. Then you'll see how to catch flies."

"How?"

"Don't tell them any more," Mackenzie said, nudging Albert. "They'll never guess."

Ruth Anne looked at Mackenzie. "Was it Albert's idea? Is it against the rules? Albert doesn't mind cheating if he thinks he can win."

"Stop your bellyaching, Four-Eyes."

"What rules?" Mackenzie said. "There are no rules. Whoever brings in the most flies wins."

"Dr. McKay doesn't abide cheaters," Eunice said. "If he doesn't like what you did, he won't give you the prize."

"Hogwash!" Albert said. "You know you're going to lose and already you're grousing." He bumped Mackenzie's elbow with his cast. The two boys grinned at each other and started down the street again.

THE POST OFFICE was across First Avenue from the Canadian Northern Railway Station. Three brightly painted, horse-drawn buses, each from a different hotel, waited in front of the depot. As the boys made their way along the sidewalk, they could hear the cab drivers calling to travellers leaving the station. Suddenly Albert held his arm out in front of Mackenzie and stopped.

A woman appeared from between two buses and began to walk slowly across the intersection. She wore a blue dress, a black veil and a feather boa that hung below her hands.

"Do you know who that is?" Albert asked.

"I've seen her before," Mackenzie said. "I remember. She was at *The Daily Phoenix* office. She's a fortune teller."

"Her name is Madame La Claire," Albert said. "She comes to our house every week. My mother says that she's better than anyone she ever consulted in Minneapolis, Minnesota."

"What does she do?"

"She reads tea leaves. She looks at my mother's hands and in her eyes. She knows things that have happened in the past. And she can tell your future."

Madame La Claire passed in front of the boys and climbed the Post Office steps.

"You don't believe that, do you?" Mackenzie asked. "It's all malarkey. Fortune tellers just make up stories."

"Not according to my mother," Albert said. "She believes everything. You know what, Mack? I bet Madame La Claire knows if my father will sell that land. And if we're going to move back to Minneapolis, Minnesota." Albert dug in his trousers pockets. "Dash it!" he muttered. "Nothing. Not a plugged nickel."

A man coming out of the Post Office held the door open for Madame La Claire and tipped his hat to her. She nodded to the man and stepped into the building.

"That's it," Albert said. "I'll ask my father for the wages he owes me. Then I'll talk to Madame La Claire and find out for sure what's going to happen."

"You'll waste your money," Mackenzie said. "You should save it for the Fair." How could the fortune teller know if someone is going to buy that land, Mackenzie asked himself. Even Mr. Crawley doesn't know that.

LIKE A DRAGONFLY AT REST, the aeroplane sat in front of the grandstand, its cloth-covered double wings held stiffly at its sides. Smaller sheets of fabric, held in place by posts and cables, were like a head at the front of the craft and a tail at the rear. Wearing an outfit of leather – boots, leggings, jacket, gloves and cap – Mr. Martin sat on the pilot's perch with both hands gripping the wheel and a pair of bug-eyed leather goggles pushed onto his forehead.

Catching a whiff of gasoline and grease, Mackenzie pressed into the circle of men and boys that surrounded the craft. Near him, hands as gentle as those touching a church's sacred objects reached to finger the wings' fabric or caress the smooth wooden blade of the propeller. For the past ten minutes the Birdman had answered questions from these bystanders. Now Mr. Martin turned to a man waiting nearby in brown overalls and a peaked army cap.

"It's time for me to go aloft, Mr. Shannon," the Birdman said.

"Yes sir," the man replied. "I'll give her another going over."

Mackenzie had come to the Exhibition with Albert long before the grandstand show was to begin. When Mackenzie insisted on getting close to the aeroplane, Albert had drifted off to the midway.

"That's the Birdman's mechanic," someone behind Mackenzie said. "He came all the way from California with Mr. Martin."

"Stand back!" Mr. Shannon walked to the end of one double wing. "Make way for the takeoff, gentlemen."

"Where will you fly today, Mr. Martin?" one of the men in the circle asked.

"How high?" another voice added. "Will you break the record?"

"I intend to go as high as I am able," the aviator said. "How high that is will depend on the winds up there. The conditions are never the same as they are on the ground."

"What height did you reach yesterday?"

"Only about three thousand feet. There's not much to talk about until you're well over a mile. As for my route, I'll trace a figure eight over these grounds until I gain a good altitude. Then I'll set off north and follow the river to the Canadian Pacific Railway tracks. When I turn and come back over the city, I'll dip down to about eight hundred feet to give people a good look. The remainder of my flight I'll be over the grandstand, doing whatever it takes to give you folks a good show."

"What can you see when you're the Birdman?" a voice called from the other side of the ring. Mr. Martin turned.

"From two or three thousand feet I can see every crook and turn of the river for miles each way. I can't see the detail of the land when I'm that high, nothing but the wide expanse of prairie. When I'm lower down, though, I can easily inspect every field and grove of trees and every sandy island on the river. One way or another, there's nothing that can escape me."

"Have you ever taken a passenger on a flight, Mr. Martin?"

"I have, but it's not something I do as a rule. It's perfectly safe if he grips a strut tightly but I've found too many passengers lose their enthusiasm for flight, and their hold on their dinner, shortly after we leave the ground."

I won't get sick, Mackenzie told himself, when I'm a flier.

The mechanic joined the aviator again. "Everything's in order, sir," he said.

Mr. Martin pulled the goggles over his eyes and cinched the chinstrap.

"You'll have to go back to your seats, gentlemen," the mechanic said. "You can see everything from there. Mr. Martin will be taking off shortly."

The mechanic huddled with the Birdman at his perch near the front of the aeroplane as the men sauntered toward the grandstand. Mackenzie approached the craft and stroked the end of a cloth-covered wing. It isn't very big, he thought. It looked much larger on Monday when Mr. Martin flew it over the city.

Turning, Mackenzie followed those streaming past the tents of the 101 Ranch Wild West Show. Albert was waiting at the bottom of the steps into the grandstand.

"You missed a great show," he said.

"Which one did you see?"

"The dog and monkey hotel. It was hilarious. There's this little hotel that a dog and a monkey operate entirely. You never see a human on the stage at all. The clerk is a gorilla who'd scare anyone if they came near. A monkey runs the elevator. And all these dogs and monkeys show up pretending to need a place to stay for the night. I never laughed so hard! You should go."

"I might," Mackenzie said, "with my father."

"He's ready!" a man cried.

The boys turned to see Mr. Martin raise one gloved hand and point over his shoulder. The mechanic grasped the top blade and hauled it down. The engine barked, sputtered, then caught its rhythm and whipped the propeller round into a smooth blur. Backing away, the mechanic saluted Mr. Martin.

Immediately the biplane began to roll, its wings bobbing with each rut and bump in the ground. Mackenzie closed his eyes and imagined the craft lifting into the air under him. He pictured himself looking over the edge of the wing as the aeroplane

soared above the colourful tents of the Fair. Opening his eyes, Mackenzie watched the spinning propeller push the aeroplane toward the waiting clouds.

"What's next?" Albert asked.

Scowling, Mackenzie said, "We haven't seen the Birdman flying yet. His show will last about thirty minutes. Then the diving horse is on at three o'clock."

"I'll come back for that," Albert said. "First I want to see Jolly Trixie, the Fat Lady."

"Go ahead," Mackenzie said, backing up the steps to keep an eye on the aeroplane. "I'm not moving."

WHEN MACKENZIE NEXT SAW ALBERT, he was halfway to the top of the grandstand and licking the last threads of green fairy floss from a rolled paper. All around him people were settling their children, talking to neighbours and craning their necks to wave at friends in the bleachers.

"I found some seats near the top," Mackenzie yelled over the din. "Mr. Arnold said he'd watch them for us."

"Who's that?"

Albert's not even thinking about those flies anymore, Mackenzie thought. Fixing his friend in his gaze, he said, "It's the man who lives behind us. He has a horse that he keeps stabled in his yard. Remember?"

"Oh, him." Albert dropped the sticky paper into a garbage box.

Mackenzie began climbing the steps two at a time. None of the huge grandstand had been painted yet. The fresh planks smelled new like the stacks of wood in a lumberyard. Towering posts rose higher than light poles to hold up the enormous roof that sheltered the thousands of people waiting in their seats.

Halfway to the top, Mackenzie saw that Albert was lagging behind and he stopped. Tall white tents whose roofs dipped and swooped in a row of peaks like a snow-capped mountain range stretched for one hundred feet out from either end of the bleachers. The top of each of the dozens of poles supporting the tents held a colourful flag. The British Union Jack, the American Stars and Stripes and the crimson and green pennants of the 101 Ranch Wild West Show flapped weakly in the heat.

Most of the fronts of the long tents were hung with canvas but here and there a flap had been raised. From one of these openings a single horse was led by a groom onto the newly cut grass in front of the thousands of onlookers. The mare's white coat was dappled in grey and a wide leather strap was cinched around her girth. Acting as relaxed as if she were alone in her home pasture, the horse ambled across the field.

"Is it hard to climb with that cast?" Mackenzie asked when Albert reached him. "We can rest for a minute."

"It's like having a heavy blanket wrapped around your arm. Isn't there anything closer?"

"These are great seats. You won't be sorry. We'll be looking right down on the horse when she jumps."

Keeping a watch over his shoulder, Mackenzie climbed further. The horse and groom had reached a high wooden tower. A steep ramp with wooden railings rose like a staircase from the ground to a platform at the top. In front of the tower sat a tank with sides as tall as a man, built of wooden planks lined with canvas. It was full to the brim with water.

Mackenzie led Albert along a row of seats, pushing between people's knees and the backs of those in front. He faltered. The space on the plank was wide enough for two boys but somehow Eunice McMahon and Ruth Anne Hardcastle had arrived there at the same time. Eunice glared at Mackenzie. "We were here first," she said and nudged her friend from behind. "Sit down Ruth Anne."

"No you don't," Albert said. "Those are for us. They're reserved. Find your own seats." Mackenzie felt Albert's cast pressing into his back.

"Plunk yourself down," a man called from further up in the stands. "There's room for the lot of you."

Mackenzie sat and a moment later Albert pried his way between him and Mr. Arnold. When the girls squeezed in, Mackenzie found himself tight against Ruth Anne. He didn't like the feel of her body touching his side. He leaned against Albert but his friend wouldn't budge. Albert would be enjoying this, he knew. Mackenzie could already hear him calling Ruth Anne his girlfriend. "Push over," he hissed.

"Ladies and gentlemen," the announcer began, "please welcome Miss Lulu Carr and her horse Blue Belle!" Mackenzie spotted the tall, thin man wearing a black suit and a top hat that made him look even taller. Stepping onto a small platform near the first row of seats, he raised a three-foot-long megaphone to his mouth. "Miss Lulu Carr, known across the entire western plains as the bravest woman ever to ride a horse off the high tower."

Wearing a long, loose-fitting dress, Indian moccasins and a straw cowboy hat, Lulu Carr emerged through a door in one of the tents. She stopped, raised her hat and waved to the cheers and applause.

"Ladies and gentlemen," the announcer continued, "this afternoon you will watch in wonder as our courageous cowgirl leads Blue Belle onto the treacherous ramp you see before you! Without hesitation, horse and rider will climb to the highest level of this tower and there —"

"We know that's what they're going to do," a man behind Mackenzie complained. "Get on with it."

"You wouldn't be so quick if it was you about to mount that horse's back," a woman answered.

"Perhaps you'd rather do it without the poor horse," another woman teased. "Just close your eyes and jump."

"Hush up, all of you," a man chided. "We're missing what he's saying."

"When the conditions are absolutely correct," the announcer went on, "Blue Belle, with Lulu Carr astride her, will plunge through the air and fall thirty feet – thirty feet ladies and gentlemen! – into the centre of that shallow tank."

With a final wave, the cowgirl walked to the tower and, grasping a handrail, started up the ramp. The groom led the mare behind her then unclipped the lead and allowed Blue Belle to climb on her own to the top. She stopped when her front legs were about two feet from the edge of the platform. Reaching up to put her arm around the mare's neck, Lulu leaned close to Blue Belle and spoke into the horse's ear.

"You must remain absolutely silent," the announcer warned, as his voice grew softer. "It requires the total concentration of horse and rider to prepare for this incredible leap. Even the slightest miscalculation could cause them to miss the tank and fall to certain injury and perhaps death."

"That's terrible," Ruth Anne whispered. "They shouldn't make the horse do that. She could be killed." She turned toward Mackenzie. "Don't you think that's cruel?"

Mackenzie didn't answer. Making his face go blank, he pretended he hadn't heard Ruth Anne's question.

She leaned closer. "Are you going to watch? What if they miss?"

"They won't," Mackenzie muttered out of the side of his mouth. "It's a show. Don't look if you're so scared."

Ruth Anne studied Mackenzie's face. "I'm not

afraid," she said. "But you shouldn't watch just to see someone get hurt. Or worse."

Mackenzie let out his breath. "I'm watching," he said. "You can do what you want." Albert's cast jabbed into his ribs.

"Can't you two be quiet?" his friend said. "Why are you talking to her anyway?"

"I'm not," Mackenzie said, then leaned forward, elbows on his knees, until his face was almost between the shoulders of the two people sitting in front of him.

Lulu Carr climbed onto the railing on the side of the platform and sprang lightly to the mare's back. She took hold of the leather belly strap and gently rubbed her heels into the horse's sides. Blue Belle walked forward until her hooves rested on the edge of the platform. A hush settled over the grandstand as the thousands of watchers held their breath and waited. The horse lifted her head like she was sniffing the wind and curled her upper lip. Two hundred feet away, Mackenzie was sure he heard her fluttering snort.

Blue Belle lowered her long neck and swung her head to peer down to one side of the tower and then the other. Stepping her back hooves forward, she sprang.

As the horse dropped, her head lunged forward, her front legs tucked under her body as if she were springing over a fence and her hind legs and tail flew out to the rear. Lightly grasping the leather strap, Miss Lulu Carr sat straight back, her long hair floating up behind her. Horse and rider seemed to hang in the air, leaving the spectators to wonder where they would land.

Finally, Lulu and Blue Belle disappeared into a foot-high wave that spilled over the sides of the tank.

"Ooooh." The audience murmured in relief, then loudly showed its approval.

For a few moments only the heads of the horse and rider were visible over the side of the tank. Then Blue Belle climbed up a ramp and the pair emerged, water sluicing off their bodies. The groom was waiting on a platform to lead the dripping horse and rider down an incline to the ground.

"Unbelievable," Mackenzie said, turning to Albert. "They hit it like a bull's eye."

"Miss Lulu Carr!" the announcer thundered. "And her talented horse, Blue Belle! The greatest horse and rider jumping act in all of North America! Show your appreciation and wonder!"

The crowd roared. Mr. Arnold stuck two fingers between his lips and whistled. "It's a brave horse that'll do what that one did," he said. "Brave and darn smart. She was the one who decided when to jump. All the cowgirl did was go along for the ride."

"I watched," Ruth Anne said to Mackenzie. "Everything. Except I closed my eyes when they were just at the bottom. Did you?"

Mackenzie couldn't answer. If he did, Albert would never shut up about it. He turned toward Mr. Arnold.

"I saw your pie at the exhibits last night," Mackenzie said. "Third prize. Congratulations."

"Why thank you, Mack," Mr. Arnold said, getting to his feet. "I'm just off to pick up that pie. It's been admired long enough. Now it has to be eaten. Why don't you and your friend tag along."

"You bet! Come on, Albert."

And goodbye Ruth Anne and Eunice, Mackenzie thought. Sometimes it seems like every time I turn around I'm surrounded by girls.

THE DELICIOUS AROMA of apples baking in a sugary syrup filled the kitchen that evening. Usually Mackenzie would have asked his mother by now when the dessert was going to be ready, and if, before supper, he could have a spoonful of fruit dripping with the sweet liquid. But today he didn't want to talk to his mother about dessert, not after what he'd done with one of her pie plates.

Happily playing on the kitchen floor, Nellie set a clamshell in the bottom of her favourite toy, a blue tin box that had carried shortbread from the Huntley Biscuit Company in London, England. She closed the hinged lid of the box and murmured to herself. Then she opened the lid, removed the shell and carefully replaced it with a bent-handled spoon.

Mother must have noticed the missing plate by now, Mackenzie thought. Twice he'd seen her kneel down and peer deep into the drawer that held her baking pans. Sooner or later she was going to ask if he'd had anything to do with it disappearing. What was he going to say when she did?

"Hello, everyone!" Mackenzie's father called, swinging open the door.

Nellie squealed and shot up her arms. Laughing, Mackenzie's father hung his straw boater hat on a hook and reached down for his daughter.

Mackenzie sighed. I have to talk to Albert, he decided. His plan isn't going to work. Someone's going to find out what we've done long before Saturday. Besides, I'm the one who has to look after what's in our box closet. Albert isn't doing anything.

"TEA WOULD BE WONDERFUL, Maude," Mackenzie's father said, sitting back from the table after the meal and resting his elbows on the arms of his chair. "Fetch it for your mother, will you, Son?"

Mackenzie gathered up some plates and went to the kitchen. When he returned to the dining room a few minutes later, his father was speaking.

"He's tall and rather slight and all of twenty-six years old. He loves being up in his aeroplane and that's all he wants to talk about. I spent about an hour interviewing him, and whenever I asked about his personal life he changed the subject. He'd rather tell how long it takes to climb a mile above the earth. And how cold it gets up there in the heavens."

He's talking about Mr. Martin, Mackenzie thought. Father met the Birdman! Mackenzie set down the teapot and dropped into his chair. "How cold *does* it get?" he asked.

"He says that to keep warm enough to operate the aeroplane at a high altitude he wears woollen underwear under his suit of leather clothing, and sometimes overtop of all that a regular winter outfit. He has a special pair of mink-lined gloves to keep his hands comfortable. But the cold can't bother him too much. The moment he climbs down from one trip, all he wants to do is fly away again. 'I didn't have enough fun,' he says. 'I want to go higher.' Can you imagine what it would feel like to be five thousand feet up, Maude?"

"I don't care to," Mackenzie's mother said, spooning the last of Nellie's supper into the baby's mouth.

"I bet he flew that high this afternoon," Mackenzie said. "One time he kept on going up and up until he was just a tiny speck. Then he dove down like he was on a corkscrew going round and round and round. Everyone thought he was going to crash. People were screaming! Then at the last moment he straightened out his aeroplane and sailed off over the bleachers as easy as a seagull coasting on the wind."

Mackenzie felt his mother frowning at him, but he went on. "After that, we lost sight of him for awhile.

No one knew where he was. Then all of a sudden – boom! – here he was thundering over the grandstand. He can do anything with that aeroplane." Again Mackenzie saw himself piloting Mr. Martin's biplane, soaring over buildings, racing up to the clouds. Before he could stop himself, he blurted out, "That's all I want to do. I want to fly like the Birdman."

Mackenzie's mother sat back in her chair and stared hard at his father. When she spoke, her words came slowly, as if she wanted to be sure each one was understood. "I think," she began, "that both of you are forgetting about all the accidents we read about with these flying machines. They are by no means safe. It seems not a week goes by that there isn't a report in your newspaper about one of those aeroplanes falling from the sky. I'm sure that it was less than a month ago, Ted, that *The Daily Phoenix* showed pictures of that mishap that killed poor Harriet Quimby. And she was an experienced pilot. She'd flown over the English Channel."

"It's because they're still so new, Maude," Mackenzie's father said, reaching for the teapot. "Three and a half years, that's all it's been since Mr. Bell's Silver Dart first flew in Nova Scotia. I'm sure that every day the pilots are getting better."

"And Mr. Martin's one of the best, isn't he, Father? He's never crashed once." Mackenzie liked being on the same side as his father. It was like when they visited Mr. Brittner's store and never told his mother.

"No, apparently not. A few close calls, that's all. He says a pilot has to know that the most dangerous times are when the craft is taking off or landing. That's when he has to be especially careful, or he could quickly tumble into the ground."

"Enough, Ted," Mackenzie's mother said. "I don't want to hear any more stories about aeroplanes." She wiped Nellie's face and turned to Mackenzie. "I know you think you'd like to fly on one some day," she said. "But for now I can't abide the idea." She sipped her tea. "I can't imagine what it would take to convince me to allow you onto one of those contraptions."

"When I'm older –"

"No, please," Mackenzie's mother said, "let's find something else for us to talk about. Mr. Martin's been here for two days, Ted. What does he think of our city?"

Mackenzie's father's face clouded. "He enjoyed the welcome he received, but that changed this afternoon. When I interviewed him he had just returned from his second flight to find that some thief had been in his hotel room. The robber seemed to know what he was looking for, something mighty precious to Mr. Martin. Mr. Flanagan was very upset that that could happen in his establishment. He offered to pay for whatever had been stolen. But from what Mr. Martin said, it isn't replaceable."

"What was it?" Mackenzie asked.

"He wouldn't say. He's told the police, I suppose, but no one else. He still likes our city, though. And he'll finish his shows."

Who would do that? Mackenzie wondered. Who would even know what was in his hotel room?

"That's very unfortunate," Mackenzie's mother said. "And I'm glad he won't be deserting us. From all that I've heard, he's a marvellous showman. But there's something completely different I wanted to ask you about, Ted. I had a bit of a disagreement with Mrs. Armsbitter yesterday. We were discussing this new law that prohibits white women from working in Chinese restaurants. It seems too harsh."

"A Chinese restaurant owner in Moose Jaw has already been convicted," Mackenzie's father said. "He's going to appeal that ruling, but for now the law stands. Chief Dunning says the police are going to start enforcing the law here, too."

"Why don't the police stop picking on Chinese people?" Mackenzie said. "They're not hurting anybody."

"The police can do only what the law says," his father said. "I think that they try to be fair. That was certainly the case in a story I wrote today. The police wasted no time in charging a couple of ne'er-do-wells who attempted to sneak a free meal from a Chinese café."

But the police say Chinese people steal things, Mackenzie thought. That's what Albert said. And Mrs. Armsbitter doesn't want them to hire whoever they want. And still Jin and his uncle keep being nice to people. "If I was Chinese," he said, "that would make me angry."

Mackenzie's father looked his way. "I don't think getting angry would help much," he said. "There are so few Chinese that it wouldn't make any difference." Turning back to Mackenzie's mother he rubbed his palms together and said, "I have something completely different on my mind, too, Maude. Didn't I smell baked apple when I came home?"

"Yes!" Mackenzie's mother clapped her hands. "I forgot. Mackenzie, the pan is cooling on the stovetop. Please bring it to the table. You know, that's the strangest thing. I always use my pie plates to bake the apples, but today one of them was missing."

Mackenzie knew what was coming. Pushing himself to his feet, he grabbed Nellie's bowl and spoon and made a beeline for the kitchen. As he slipped through the door, he heard his mother say, "I had intended on making a double recipe and giving some to Betty Armsbitter. Have you seen one of my tin pie plates, Ted?"

Mackenzie dipped a finger into the sweet, warm syrup puddled on the bottom of the pan and stuck it in his mouth. Delicious! He put his finger in again. If he waited for a minute or so, his parents might be talking about something different when he returned.

CLAIM PRICES IN RESTAURANT WERE TOO HIGH

Penniless Young Men Try for Free Meal

Two young men who accompanied several others into a local restaurant on Twentieth Street East after a day at the Exhibition yesterday kicked up a row when payment for what they had eaten became due. Although the young men became vehement in their arguments, the Chinese owner of the establishment stood firm. In a shorter time than it takes to tell, a large crowd assembled outside the restaurant while quite a number stepped inside to hear what was going on.

The young fellows claimed they were charged too much for what was ordered, but the facts of the matter are that the two were penniless and unable to pay. Before ordering they were perfectly aware how much they were liable for, as the prices were printed in black and white on the menu.

Besides curious bystanders, the hubbub also drew the attention of a passing police officer who wasted little time in rounding up the two shysters and escorting them to a free bed where they awaited their appearance in today's police court.

CHAPTER FOUR
Thursday, August 8, 1912

NELLIE GRIPPED THE RIM OF HER YELLOW SUN hat and lifted it up so the ribbon caught beneath her chin. She fussed with the hat – left and right, up and down – until it flopped over her head and fell to the ground in the garden. A few yards away her mother was on her hands and knees picking weeds. Setting her sights on a row of carrots, Nellie teetered over lines of onions and leafy beets.

Mackenzie rested the handle of a hoe against his shoulder, lifted his cap from his head and wiped the sleeve of his shirt across his face. It was still morning and already the temperature was in the nineties. A cloud of grey dust swirled up his pant leg and settled on his shoulders. Mackenzie sneezed. He only liked helping his mother in the spring when the soil still smelled sweet and moist and each shovelful brought earthworms slithering to the surface. Catching sight of the knife gash in his boot, Mackenzie dragged his foot across the newly hoed soil and used his heel to press dirt into the cut. He patted his trouser pocket. His knife was there, as usual. But it would be gone if his mother ever spotted that hole.

"Nellie!" his mother cried. "Mackenzie, you have to watch her. Don't let her do that." Somehow Nellie had been able to pull out a carrot with each hand. Fixing her eyes on Mackenzie, she jammed one of the dirty vegetables into her mouth.

Dropping the hoe, Mackenzie leapt to his sister. Nellie wailed while Mackenzie wiped both carrots on the leg of his trousers.

"Look at her face!" his mother said. "I swear she could be a little gopher. If she wants a carrot, you need to wash it. There's a basin on the stoop." Grimacing, she asked, "Where's that stench coming from? There's been a very unpleasant odour in our yard the last couple of days."

Mackenzie sniffed the air on the way to the steps but didn't turn around. "I can't smell anything," he said. "Nellie, just wait. I'll bring them right back."

"You can't? It's quite strong." His mother looked toward the back alley. "I wonder if it isn't Mr. Arnold's manure pile. It's been awhile since he had it removed. If it gets worse, I'm going to have to mention it to him." She waved her hand in front of her face. "And all of these flies! Surely you've noticed that."

"Uh...I suppose so. There are always a few of them around." Mackenzie handed the carrots to his sister.

83

"This is considerably more than a few! I swear, you and your father. Sometimes it's like you can't see what's right in front of your noses. Look. Two of them just landed on Nellie's hand." Mackenzie's mother shoved her trowel into the ground. "That's it. Grab that little rascal, Mackenzie. It's time to clean her up anyway. I have some shopping to do on Broadway Avenue."

Mackenzie shooed the flies away from his sister then looked over her head toward the box closet. Albert's plan was turning into a real mess. *I can't leave that stuff there until Saturday,* he decided. *What if all these flies make Nellie sick again? That's not worth my five-dollar share of the prize.*

HENRY LAVALLÉE'S familiar shiny green rig was parked on the edge of the street while Stanley wiped its side with a thin cloth he'd dipped in a horse trough. Mackenzie waited until his mother had entered Moffat's Meat Market, then parked his sister's pram beside the store and joined his friend.

"Where's Henry Lavallée?" he asked.

"He is in there," Stanley said, nodding across the boardwalk to the Allwood Harness and Confectionery. "We will deliver them some saddles this afternoon. First we must take this load to the Exhibition."

"What have you got this time?" Mackenzie asked, looking over the side of the wagon.

The dray was loaded from front to back. Fifty-pound bags held flour and oats and sugar. Wooden boxes, some of them stamped "Eggs Fragile," were stacked four high. Along one side stood large metal cans like the ones farmers used to ship their milk into the city on the train.

"It is for the canteen of the Wild West Show," Stanley said.

"They'll eat all that?" As he spoke Mackenzie saw Henry Lavallée leave the harness shop.

"Yes," Stanley said. "We took a full wagon yesterday already. Now we must take it again."

"That's a heap of food!"

"It is like a little village they are feeding out there," Henry Lavallée said, resting his arm on a wheel. "They have more than one hundred and fifty people. It does not take them long to go through a pile of grub like this." Rubbing a thick, calloused finger under his beret, the teamster added, "Look at that fellow."

Mackenzie turned to see a man riding a bicycle down Broadway Avenue clutching the handlebar with one hand. In the crook of his other arm he held a few sheets of glass bundled together with twine.

"I know him," Henry Lavallée said. "He has a homestead about twenty-five miles east of here. Last summer I took a load of lumber to him. He and his family were living in a tent then. He built his house before winter but he couldn't afford to put in the windows, so they stayed boarded over. Now, I see, he has the glass."

"He's going to carry it on his bicycle for twenty-five miles?" Mackenzie asked. "There's just a wagon trail out there. What if he falls?"

"He will try very hard not to fall." Henry Lavallée chuckled. "If he does, they will have to wait another year to see the sun inside their house."

"I hope he makes it," Mackenzie said. "It'd be terrible not to have any windows."

"We must go now, Stanislav," Henry Lavallée said, pulling himself onto the wagon. "We do not want to keep the hungry cowboys waiting for their meal." Stanley sprang to the seat.

"You might see my father," Mackenzie said. "He's going to write a story about the Wild West Show."

"We will watch for him," Henry Lavallée said, nodding at his helper.

"Giyup," Stanley snapped the reins, the harness jangled, the wooden tongue creaked and the wagon jerked forward.

Further down Broadway Avenue, Mackenzie spotted Albert walking toward him beside a woman. It was Madame La Claire! His friend was taking long strides to keep up with the fortune teller, swinging his right arm and keeping his cast tucked against his chest. As they got closer, Mackenzie heard the woman say, "It is not so simple, what you ask. To know the future, Madame must understand his past. Madame must learn the little secrets that guide his life."

"I just want to know one thing," Albert said,

passing in front of Mackenzie without looking his way. "That's all."

I know what he wants, Mackenzie thought. But it's nothing she can tell him.

"You are so young," the fortune teller said. "You do not understand. Life is never one thing or another thing. It is a mystery." She smiled at Albert. "Life is not always what it seems to be. The truth is hidden by illusions."

That won't make him happy.

"It won't take you long," Albert said, tugging at her sleeve.

"Here?" Madame La Claire stopped suddenly and threw her arm toward the street. "You think Madame can talk of such things *here*, with horses and motor cars, with people rushing this way and that, shouting and laughing? No. That is not possible. You must come to Madame's studio or you must wait until her next sitting with your mother." The fortune teller leaned closer to Albert, took his hand in hers, and in a soft voice said, "You will answer Madame's questions." She gazed at his palm. "Madame will study the lines of your life. She sees that it is a long life and very complicated. But in time she will understand you, like she understands your mother. Everything will be known."

"No. I can't wait." Albert freed his hand and reached into his trousers pocket. "I've got my own money. I can pay you."

"Certainly not! Now you wish to insult Madame." The fortune teller turned her head to the side. "It must end here. Madame must go to her studio and you must not follow her."

Flinging the end of the boa over her shoulder, Madame La Claire raised her chin and strode across Broadway Avenue.

Mackenzie walked over to his friend. "You're being stupid to think that fortune tellers know what will happen in the future," he said. "You should just forget her."

"You wouldn't talk like that if you knew what she told my mother last night."

Mackenzie glanced at his friend. Albert sounded very serious. Did Mrs. Crawley ask about the sale of the land? he wondered. "Was it about your father?" he asked.

"No. My mother doesn't care about my father's deals." Albert slid a finger inside his cast and scratched his skin. "My mother asked about her jewellery. She was crying when she talked about it. Madame La Claire picked up some of my mother's other jewellery. She read my mother's palm and did the things she always does. Then she told my mother not to worry. Her jewellery will be found."

That's what she'd want to hear, Mackenzie thought. "That must have made your mother happy."

"Madame La Claire told my mother that her things would be found by someone she knows very well."

"Your father? Or you! Did she mean you?"

"Yes, I think so." Albert sighed. "Then Madame La Claire said that the one who finds the jewellery will soon go on a big trip. To some place very exciting."

A big trip. "Uh-oh. Does she mean you're going back to Minneapolis?"

"I don't know."

"Didn't you ask?"

"I wasn't there. Mother never allows me to be in the room when she's consulting a fortune teller. She told me later, after Madame had left. That's why I pleaded with Madame when I saw her this morning. Obviously she knows something. I don't understand why she won't just tell me."

"And your father won't say?"

"The men in Chicago don't want the land, but my father found some people in St. Louis who do. They want time to think about it. This could go on for days, Mack, or it might be all over this afternoon."

This is really bothering him, Mackenzie thought. He's not going to like what I have to tell him, either. "Albert," he said, "I'm sorry about what the fortune teller said. But I've been thinking about that fly contest. It's going to get me into trouble. I have to buy Mother a new pie plate, for one thing. And I already had to lie and say I didn't know where her old one was. I don't think she believed me. If it doesn't show up, she'll keep asking."

"Well, buy her a new one, then."

"I don't have any money. I spent it all at the Exhibition. This was your idea, Albert, but I'm doing all the work. And it's my backyard that's starting to reek like a manure pile."

"That won't last. You liked the idea too. We're partners."

"I went along with it because I felt bad that you'd fractured your wrist. But, I'm quitting."

"Not yet! It's only two more days. We'll have thousands of flies by Saturday. We'll win the prize. Then see if you want to quit."

"There are already too many flies. That's part of the problem. My mother's complaining about them. They're getting out of the box closet. They're all over the place."

"Already? That's better than I thought. We can start to capture some and save them."

"It's too late. I'm going to have to clean out that foul thing."

"No, Mackenzie. It'll be okay until Saturday. Two days! It'd be crazy to stop now."

Mackenzie had thought he was going to make Albert change his mind. He'd forgotten how stubborn his friend was. But he had to at least start to get things back to normal.

"My mother's pie plate," he said. "I have to replace it. That can't wait."

"All right, all right." Albert found a coin in his pocket and handed it over. "You'll thank me on Saturday when we win that prize," he said.

MACKENZIE FINGERED ALBERT'S MONEY as he stepped into Brittner's General Store and Used Goods Emporium later that morning. The shoeshine named Fletcher was bent over the feet of a sunburned man sitting in his chair. The man's young son stood by his side. Bauer slouched in the other stand, his eyes closed and his chin resting on his chest. Twisting around, Fletcher sized up Mackenzie. Then he turned to his job. The customer looked uncomfortable, as if he would rather be back on his farm with his worn boots sunk into a freshly ploughed field.

"We're in town for just a couple of days," the farmer said, ruffling his son's hair. "My wife's been anxious to take in the Fair. She received a bit of an inheritance and she's determined to see it spent on some of the latest marvels. Our hotel room already looks like a London shop. I can't think what more she'll bring home today." He chuckled. "The boy and I will get a close look at some of those amusement rides. That's more our style."

"The hotels are bursting at their seams right now," Fletcher said as Mackenzie walked past breathing in the leathery smell. "Where did you manage to find a bed?"

"The Empress. It's a little out of the way on the east side, but quieter than some."

"You were smart to come here to get a proper shine," Fletcher said. "You won't regret it. You start to treat these shoes kindly after this and all they'll need is a quick buff on a Sunday morning." With a flick of his wrist, Fletcher cracked his cloth, frightening the boy and driving him against his father's leg. "We get a steady stream in here during the Exhibition," the shoeshine said. "Even the Birdman made this one of his first stops in the city."

Mackenzie smiled at the mention of Mr. Martin. He was going to get another close look at the Birdman's aeroplane that afternoon.

Perched on his stool, Mr. Brittner looked up from the customer facing him across his cabinet. Following Mackenzie with his eyes, he massaged the bumps on his bald head as if that would help him remember when he had seen this boy before. He turned, spoke quietly to the customer, and touched one of the items laid out on the countertop between them. Mackenzie stopped in front of a long table strewn with a jumble of things used in kitchens and home workshops.

When he had visited this store with his father, Mackenzie had spotted stacks of baking bowls and oven pans. Lifting one pile, he found a half-dozen dusty pie plates. He shuffled through the plates to find the least-used one. Did Mother's pie plate have all of these lines scratched into the bottom? he wondered. Was it shinier than this one? Were the sides slanted like this, or were they straighter? I'll wash it, he told himself, but she'll still know it's not the same one.

Mackenzie walked over to the cabinet and stopped a few feet from the man who was now talking in a whisper with the storekeeper. After studying the hand-guns displayed under the glass top, he let his eyes wander over to what Mr. Brittner was showing the customer. Mackenzie's breath caught in his throat.

"A.B.C." The initials were engraved into the gold cover of a pocket watch. Albert B. Crawley. Many times Mackenzie had seen Albert's father take that watch from his vest pocket, snap open the cover and announce the time. He stared at the other items sitting on the glass. There were at least ten watches. Nearby were some men's and women's rings. In a separate pile Mackenzie spotted some jewelled necklaces. A lone tie pin with a red stone in the centre lay by Mr. Brittner's hand.

"Fine," the customer murmured. "I'll take these for now." His hand closed over five or six rings which he pulled toward him across the counter and dropped into his jacket pocket. He handed Mr. Brittner a bill.

"Excellent choices," the storekeeper said. "You're getting a good price for those." He started to gather up the items left on the counter and place them in a small wooden chest. If that *is* Albert's father's watch, Mackenzie thought, some of the other jewellery might belong to his family, too. He wanted to reach out and grab everything in the chest. I'll tell them they made a mistake, he thought. Before he could think what to say, the customer spoke.

"It's busier than a picnic on an anthill out there," the man complained, looking out the front windows. "There must be a copper on every corner."

That's an odd thing to say, Mackenzie thought. Most people like having the police around.

"It's on account of the Exhibition," Mr. Brittner said. "But come back this afternoon. The mayor made it a holiday. He wants all the shops closed so everyone can visit the Fair. Won't be a soul in these parts." The storekeeper reached behind him and lifted a key from a hook on the wall near the cash register. "I'll let you out the back door," he said. "I've a few more things I can show you."

When he turned to find Mackenzie at the end of the cabinet, Mr. Brittner seemed startled.

"How long have you been there?" he asked.

"Those watches –" Mackenzie began.

"What about them?" Mr. Brittner kept his eyes on Mackenzie as his hand swept up the remaining jewellery.

"Uh...I thought I recognized one of them."

"No. Not these." Mr. Brittner dropped the last piece into the wooden chest and closed its lid. "These are new stock. Imported. Not what you're likely to find around here." He tapped the end of his finger onto the glass top. "These are the second-hand ones. You might have seen anyone wearing them before they decided to sell to me." He nodded at Mackenzie's hand. "What have you got there?"

Holding up the tin plate, Mackenzie laid a nickel on the counter.

"You're Ted Davis's boy, aren't you? When you were here with your father I wanted you to have something that caught your eye. You like that pan? Just take it.

You don't have to pay me." Mr. Brittner wrapped his hand around the chest and lifted it off the counter.

Mackenzie didn't know what to say. Maybe he had been mistaken. Maybe it was some other letters, not A.B.C., he had seen on the watch.

"Is it for your mother?"

"Yes."

"She's a fine woman, your mother. I haven't seen her for a coon's age. You tell her to drop by sometime. I'll give her a good deal on whatever she pleases. Don't you forget to come back with your father, either. One of my boys will give your Sunday shoes a good sparkle." Mr. Brittner smiled, then slid off his stool and led the customer to the back of the store.

"Thank you," Mackenzie mumbled. He took a few steps toward the front door then, slowing down, wondered if he should try again to explain about the watch to Mr. Brittner.

He decided not to when Fletcher looked up from sorting the cloths and brushes in his apron pockets and stared hard at him. The farmer and his son were gone, to the Exhibition, Mackenzie supposed. Bauer was nowhere to be seen either. Until he was right outside the store, Mackenzie could feel Fletcher's eyes boring into his back.

"HOLY SMACKERS! You saw my father's watch at Brittner's store?" Albert paced back and forth on the boardwalk in front of the ABC building. "That guy's as crooked as a snake. Everybody knows it. Father thinks Mr. Brittner gives all of us Americans a bad name. He says he's like a whiskey trader, like those men who used to come up from stateside and sell bad liquor to the Indians."

"I can't be sure," Mackenzie said. He was sitting on the steps to the office with his arms resting on his knees and his cap pushed back on his forehead. "I thought I saw it. But I might have been wrong. I didn't get a really good look."

"What about Mother's things? Did you see any ladies' jewellery?"

"Some, but he packed them up too quickly."

"In what? Mother keeps her jewellery in a little wooden chest..." Albert held up his hands as if he was holding an invisible box.

"I don't know, Albert. It was just one of those things ladies use to keep their jewellery. Have you ever been in his place?"

"Never. It's just a junk store, right?"

"Pretty much. There was nothing fancy that I saw. It was mostly gear that people wouldn't want anymore"

"What about the jewellery? Where was it?"

"There was some in a cabinet near the cash register. And I think he has a storeroom for that sort of thing at the back. The man I told you about who bought the rings? Mr. Brittner was taking him there to look at more stuff."

"Of course. He'd keep the stolen goods separately, not out in the open with the junk. If we're going to find my father's watch, we have to get into that room, Mack. My mother's things, too. How are we going to do that?"

"Albert, not so fast. I might have been mistaken. He said I was. And my father likes him. He says Mr. Brittner's odd but he wouldn't hurt anyone. Or steal anything. I should just go back and ask him to let me see the watch. He might show me and then we'd know for sure."

"Are you crazy? He'd know we're on to him."

"Then we should tell the police."

"I want to be the one to find those things, Mack. I want to take them to my parents. If my mother has her jewellery back and my father gets his watch, they're not going to want to leave town so badly." Albert sat down beside Mackenzie. "Tell me everything you know about that place. Then we'll make a plan. Brittner's not very smart. This'll be a snap. You'll see."

"Well, there *is* a key to the back door –" Mackenzie started.

"Oh, great!" Albert was staring at the opposite side of the street. "What does your girlfriend want? Tell her to get lost."

Mackenzie turned to see Eunice and Ruth Anne walking across the street toward them.

"She's not my girlfriend."

Ruth Anne smiled, then looked down to fidget with her cloth handbag, sliding the handles back and forth between her elbow and her wrist.

"We're not going in that contest," Eunice said. "It's too dirty having to kill flies and then pick them up and store them. Flies are revolting."

"Sometimes you have to get dirty," Albert said, "if you're going to make a little money. What are you doing with the ones you caught?"

"They're in a bottle behind my father's store," Eunice said, wrinkling her nose. "You can have them if you want."

"How many are there?"

"One hundred and sixteen."

"It's hardly worth it. Look, we're really busy right now. Why don't you girls vamoose."

"I told you they'd be rude," Eunice said. "We'll find someone else who wants those flies."

"Are you going to the Exhibition, Mackenzie?" Ruth Anne asked. "Where are you sitting?"

Oh, brother! What if Albert is right, Mackenzie thought. What if Four-Eyes *does* like me? I absolutely am not going to have a girlfriend.

THE DOWNTOWN STREETS were quiet that afternoon. On their way along Third Avenue, Mackenzie and Albert caught up to an empty Queens Hotel taxi before the horses turned toward the C. N. Station. A lone motor car puttered by on its way to the Traffic Bridge.

"We turn down here," Mackenzie said. The dirt

lane was rutted with wagon tracks. Boards broken from wooden crates and kegs rested against the brick buildings. Partway down the lane, the boys stopped at a door with a one-word sign nailed to the frame. "Brittner" it read.

Albert tried the doorknob. "Locked." Shifting his cast inside its sling, he studied a tiny window set in the wall above the door. "And that's too high. But you know where he keeps the key. I say we go get it."

"I still think we should ask him first. That's better than stealing his key."

"I'll steal the key, Mack. You just have to draw his attention."

"It's the same thing. Anyway, you can hardly sneak around while you're wearing that cast, let alone run if you have to."

"Let's get going," Albert said. "I want to see what this place looks like."

A "CLOSED" SIGN hung in the front window of the second-hand store, but the door was ajar. After watching Albert step into the building, Mackenzie crouched down to hear what happened.

"I'm closed!" Mr. Brittner's voice was so near, Mackenzie thought he must be sitting in one of the shoeshine chairs. The pages of a newspaper collapsed noisily.

"Boy! Didn't you hear me? The store is closed."

"The door was open." Albert's voice came from far inside the store. Mackenzie waited for a few moments then peered through the opening. Mr. Brittner was lumbering toward the back of the building where Albert had already picked up something from a table. The storekeeper's arms hung at his sides. In one hand he held the crumpled newspaper.

Mackenzie crept into the store and crouched behind one of the shoeshine chairs. "I want to buy something," he heard Albert say.

I have to see this, Mackenzie thought. Keeping low, he dashed across the store and behind Mr. Brittner's glass-topped cabinet.

"Kid, any other day you'd be welcome to spend your money in here. But not today. I've got important business to do and I don't need you in the way."

"This," Albert said. "How much do you want for this?"

Mackenzie checked around the end of the cabinet. Albert was holding a grey telescope tube about as big around as one of Henry Lavallée's fingers. Slowly he pulled the sections apart to their full length. Then, pushing one end against his cast, he snapped them back together. "I'm going out hunting gophers," Albert said. "I could use one of these."

Mr. Brittner stood across the table from Albert, his hands resting on hips. "Are you listening to me?" he growled.

Carefully placing his hands and feet one in front of the other, Mackenzie crawled along behind the cabinet until he was sure the cash register was on the counter above him.

"It can't be worth very much," Albert said. "The lens is scratched."

"You're starting to bother me, boy. I want you out of here."

"Do you have any other ones?"

What nerve, Mackenzie thought. Albert isn't flinching. Now it's my turn. He better not be looking. Mackenzie took a breath, stood up, slipped the back door key off the hook and dropped down to the floor. He exhaled. There was no sound from Mr. Brittner. He must not have been seen. After a quick peek, Mackenzie scampered on tiptoes past the shoeshines' chairs and out the door. He ran across the street and safely into a narrow opening between two buildings before he stopped and looked back toward the store.

Albert ran out with the storekeeper on his heels and leapt into the dirt street. Landing roughly, he staggered to keep from falling on his cast.

"And stay out!" Mr. Brittner tramped back into his shop and slammed the door closed.

Gripping the telescope in his right hand, Albert steadied himself and loped down the street.

"Good work!" Mackenzie said as Albert squeezed past. "Do you think he saw me?"

"Not a chance. He was looking at me the whole time. But I couldn't have kept it up much longer. I was running out of things to say." Albert laughed.

"You were making him angry. Did he try to grab you?"

"No. He was as grumpy as a porcupine and about as fast. But when I paid him I didn't risk getting too close. I just tossed him the money and took off."

"How much?"

"Ten cents. It's a deal. The telescope's not very big, but it works. It's just a little scratch."

"And I got the jackpot," Mackenzie said, holding out the key to his friend. "Now we just have to wait."

Albert leaned against a wall, tucked the telescope into his sling, and slid down onto his haunches.

"Has your father sold that land?" Mackenzie asked.

"Yep. St. Louis is going to wire the money today. It hasn't arrived yet, but it will."

"And do your parents still want to leave?"

"Yes." He held up the key. "But this could change everything."

"There he is!" Mackenzie whispered.

"Who? Is Brittner leaving?"

"No. The man who was buying things this morning. He's come back."

Albert shuffled toward the end of the building and looked across the street. "More waiting," he muttered. "I can't stand this much longer."

But it was thirty minutes later when Mackenzie announced, "They're going! Both of them." Albert got to his feet. "Mr. Brittner's closing the door," Mackenzie said. "Now he's locking it. Get your head back in so they don't spot us."

WHEN THEY STARTED down the back lane, an orange and white cat jumped from a doorstep and, tail held high, sauntered ahead of the boys as if leading them on a walk. Twenty feet along the alley, the cat slunk over to a building, dipped through a basement window and disappeared.

While Mackenzie stood watch, Albert pushed the key into the lock, turned it and opened the door. They scrambled inside and Albert slid the lock. The air smelled stale and dusty and the only light came from the dirt-stained window in the back wall.

"I can't see a thing," Albert said.

The boys stood still until Mackenzie spotted a string hanging from the ceiling. When he tugged on it, a single electric bulb lit the room.

The half-dozen crates spread across the floor looked the kinds of wooden boxes people used to pack their belongings when they moved. Each one, the boys saw, held things loosely wrapped in brown paper. Mackenzie spotted a china teapot, a miniature coal oil lantern and a silver serving platter still gleaming from its last polishing. On the walls behind the crates, small wooden boxes, some with carved sides or painted lids, lined a few rough shelves. A long-handled shovel and a pickaxe stood propped in a dim corner near the door.

"Mack!" Albert cried. "Did you ever see such a heap of loot? Where do you want to start?" Without waiting for an answer, Albert pulled a handful of paper from the nearest crate and dropped it on the floor. He plunged his good arm into the container.

Mackenzie peered through the open doorway into the dimly lit storefront. Shadows blanketed the tops of the tables and filled the spaces between them. Near the windows, the raised chairs sat empty in the sunlight. Drawing the door partway closed, Mackenzie walked over to another box. He began to take out, unwrap and set on the floor beside him bowls and teapots, brass bedpans and fancy tin boxes.

"This is going to make a big mess," Mackenzie said, looking at the pile of crumpled papers growing around Albert's legs.

"Doesn't matter," Albert said, his head deep in the crate. "We have to find that stuff."

"Do you really think that all of these were stolen?"

"Yep."

Albert straightened up, chose another box and began ripping loose paper from its top.

"Don't stop, Mack."

Mackenzie picked up a ball of paper, unwrapped it and found a pair of ceramic dolls inside. He set them carefully at his feet. If I was Mr. Brittner, he told himself, I sure wouldn't like to have people doing this in the back of my store.

A few minutes later Mackenzie was reaching for the last few things at the bottom of the crate when, "Snap!" Albert suddenly called. "Here it is." Albert held up a gold pocket watch by its chain to get a good look at the case. "A.B.C.," he said. "You were right! There are rings here, too."

"Are they your father's?"

Albert emptied a dark blue cloth bag into his palm. "Some of these might be. He has ones he never wears. I'm going to take them all, just in case." Refilling the bag, Albert cinched the top closed with a yellow cord. "Father's going to be mighty pleased when he sees these," he said.

"Albert!" Mackenzie whispered. "There's someone coming in the front door!" He reached up to tug off the light bulb, then darted past Albert to push the storeroom door closed. "We have to get out of here."

The room filled with light again. Albert walked away from the cord and along a set of shelves where he raised and closed the lid of each wooden chest in turn.

"Albert, we can't stay here. We'll come back, if you want."

"I'm not leaving without my mother's jewellery." Albert held up a necklace. "I don't remember exactly what all of it looks like. But I'll know it when I see it."

A man spoke close by in the store. "He's not back yet. We'll have to wait for him." Mackenzie recognized Bauer's voice.

"What did you find in that sodbuster's hotel room?" That was Fletcher.

"What a waste of time that was," Bauer answered. "The guy was talking through his hat. There wasn't anything worth lifting that I could see."

"What does the old man need us for this time?" Fletcher asked. "I want to get out to the races, make a little money on the horses."

"He didn't say. But he was supposed to be here by now."

"It's the two shoeshines," Mackenzie hissed. "These guys are mean. You haven't seen them. They could get really nasty if they find us here."

Albert wasn't listening. He was acting like Mackenzie's father in a hardware store, looking at every little thing as if he had all the time in the world.

"They'll see the light, sure as heck," Mackenzie said. "We have to leave!"

"I think –" Albert said. Then, "Got it!" He had the blue bag and the telescope tucked deep into his sling and in his right hand he held a wooden chest. "Everything. I'm sure of it."

About time, Mackenzie thought. Keeping his eye on the door to the store, he edged toward the back.

"You know what this means, Mackenzie," Albert whispered. "The fortune teller was right. Well, half right. I found my mother's jewellery. But when I get these things home, there'll be no more talk of moving back to Minneapolis, Minnesota." Carefully turning the key to slip the lock, Albert opened the back door a crack. "Coast's clear," he said. "Let's go!" He pulled on the door, sprang to the ground and vanished down the lane.

Mackenzie couldn't move. At the top of a crate that neither of them had looked into, he had spotted a glistening silver bar about as wide as two fingers and eight inches long that shone out from a bundled white towel. He reached for it and found the bar heavier than he expected and decorated along the edges with sparkling jewels. As he lifted it from the box he saw that a second bar was attached below the first.

It's a model, Mackenzie thought. A little aeroplane made from silver. When he spotted "The Birdman" engraved across the top wing, he knew whose it was. Mackenzie clutched the model and its towel wrapping to his chest. No wonder it's not replaceable, he thought. It must be worth a ton of money.

Mackenzie caught a glimpse of the inside door swinging toward him and the thunderstruck look on Bauer's face.

"What the –" the shoeshine blurted.

In three steps Mackenzie reached the back door and launched himself into the alley.

"Fletcher!" Bauer yelled. "That kid's in here. Quick! Get him!"

Gripping the model with one hand and fiercely pumping his other arm, Mackenzie took off down the alley.

Before he'd gone ten yards, he knew that he was in trouble. The model was weighing him down. Fletcher was right behind him. The sound of the man sucking in his breath was so close Mackenzie expected the shoeshine's grip on his arm at any moment. He threw back his head and willed himself to go faster.

At that moment a green laundry bag floated across the opening at the end of the lane.

Jin!

The pole came next, then Jin, and then the second bag. The Chinese boy halted. Turning to face the two runners, he swung the bags one in front of the other along the side of the alley.

Mackenzie's lungs hurt and his aching legs were beginning to weaken. As he closed in on Jin, he saw the Chinese boy wrap both hands around the pole in front of him.

Mackenzie knew what his friend was thinking. No! he wanted to call. Don't do it! But he couldn't find the breath. Everything he had, he needed to keep running.

Galloping past, he saw Jin fling the front bag at Fletcher.

The shoeshine swore. Mackenzie heard him fall heavily to the ground and a second later the sound of splintering wood. At the far side of the deserted street Mackenzie peeked over his shoulder and immediately stopped.

Fletcher had a grip on Jin's wrist. With a sweep of his arm, the shoeshine twisted the Chinese boy's hand behind his back and up toward his shoulder blade. Jin lurched forward as his head jerked down sharply. Mackenzie knew how much that could hurt when two boys were just wrestling for fun. Fletcher barked something at Jin. His friend reached down for one of the bags. The shoeshine looked over Jin's shoulder and across the street, his eyes drilling into Mackenzie. Fletcher grabbed the other bag in his free hand and pushed Jin down the alley.

Mackenzie looked both ways along the empty street. Albert got clean away, he decided. But what's Fletcher up to? I thought he might punch Jin for helping me escape. Why's he taking him to the store? What's he going to do with him? I can't leave Jin with those shoeshines. It's my fault he was caught.

Clutching the model through the towel, Mackenzie jogged toward Flanagan's Hotel. I'll leave this for Mr. Martin, he thought, and be back in no time flat.

THE CLERK GINGERLY UNWRAPPED the white towel across his desk, flattening one end to show the words, "Hotel Flanagan."

"Hmmm," he said, pausing to look closely at Mackenzie. "How do you happen to have one of our establishment's towels?"

"Someone stole it. Not me. Look what's inside."

The clerk spread open the rest of the towel. His eyes widened at the sight of the silver aeroplane. Resting his hands on the edge of the desk, he leaned forward until his nose almost touched the model. The man's dark hair, Mackenzie saw, was parted to expose a line of white skin that divided the top of his head evenly in two.

Peering across his desk, the clerk asked, "Do you know what this is?"

"Yes. It belongs to Mr. Martin."

"How did you get it?"

"I found it. I want to give it back."

"Do you now?" The clerk straightened up and looked across the lobby of the hotel. "What's your name? I'm sure Mr. Flanagan would like to thank you." The man sidled around the corner of his desk, his arm sliding through the air toward Mackenzie like a snake after its prey.

"Mackenzie Davis." Realizing what the clerk was up to, Mackenzie backed away. "I know who stole it," he said.

"Well, well," the clerk said. "I'm sure Chief Dunning would like to speak with you, as well. He was here just a moment ago."

"They took my friend," Mackenzie said, stepping backwards again. "I can't wait."

"Yes you *will*!" The clerk lunged, swung his arm and missed.

Mackenzie darted out of the lobby, flew down the front steps of the hotel and dashed down the street.

THE ALLEY WAS DESERTED. All that remained was Jin's pole, split like Albert's fractured wrist and abandoned against the side of a building.

What's going on? Mackenzie wondered. *Is* everything

in those crates stolen? Does Mr. Brittner know that? Fletcher said they were waiting for him to come back. Then what are they going to do? Mackenzie looked down the lane. Has Fletcher done something with Jin? What if he gets hurt because he helped me? Unless he just wanted to scare him. Mackenzie knew he had to find out.

Keeping close to the backs of the buildings and checking over his shoulder every few seconds to see if anyone was following, Mackenzie crept toward the closed door to Brittner's shop. He veered across the lane and held his ear against the wood. Hearing nothing, Mackenzie gripped the handle and turned. Expecting the door to be locked, he was surprised to see it swing away from the latch. With the tip of his finger, Mackenzie pushed the door the rest of the way open.

In the sunlight that poured in from the alley, Mackenzie could see the open crates, the piles of things set aside by himself and Albert and the sheets of wrapping paper littering the floor. At first it looked like nothing had changed. Then he spotted Jin slumped on the floor in a far corner, his eyes staring over the cloth pulled tightly across his mouth.

"Holy smoke!" After looking both ways down the lane, Mackenzie stepped inside. He walked to the middle of the room and pulled on the light bulb cord. Jin's hands were tied at the wrists with a horse's leather lead.

"They can't do this to you," Mackenzie said. "I'm letting you out."

Groaning, Jin shook his head quickly from side to side. "No!" he seemed to be saying. "No!"

"Hold on. I'll take that out of your mouth." Mackenzie reached behind Jin's head and dug his fingers into the knot. "This is a shoeshine rag! It's filthy!" Mackenzie tugged at the ends of the cloth and it fell to the floor.

"You stupid little younker."

Mackenzie spun around to find Fletcher smirking at him, his thumbs hooked into the pockets of his leather apron.

"I told him you'd be back. I knew your little Chinaman friend would be like a pot of honey drawing a fly. That's why I made sure his mouth was gagged up good."

"You –" Mackenzie's voice caught. "You have to let him go."

"Look around, kid," the shoeshine sneered. "I don't have to do anything."

"Well, I will." Mackenzie spun around but before he could touch the strap binding his friend's hands he felt his own wrist caught and wrenched up his back. Crying out, Mackenzie staggered forward. Fletcher twisted Mackenzie's arm to the front and, like a cowboy tying a steer's legs at a roundup, quickly bound his two hands together. The shoeshine grabbed Mackenzie's shoulders and shoved him to the floor beside Jin.

"We've got some business to take care of," Fletcher said. "Me and the two of you. I don't take kindly to being tripped up and made a fool of by a couple of young brats. You're not going anywhere until I've taken a strip off of both of you."

"Where's Mr. Brittner?" Mackenzie demanded. "He knows my father. He won't let you do this."

"You think Brittner's going to save you? After what you did in here? I know it was you who pawed through these boxes. I know what you took with you when you bolted off like a scared rabbit. I tell you, boy, when he finds out, it won't matter two licks who your father is. You wait. Bauer!" Fletcher called through the door to the storefront. "Come look what fell into my trap."

The second shoeshine appeared in the doorway. Slouching against the frame, he taunted Mackenzie. "Thought you were pretty smart, did you? Figured you could trick your way in here, take what you wanted, not get caught. I guess you've got something else to think about now, don't you?"

Fletcher slammed shut the back door and turned the key to slide the lock. Pulling a rag from his apron, he said, "And don't try getting noisy back here or you'll get a taste of one of these. Come on, Bauer." The men left the storeroom.

Pushing his feet against one of the crates, Mackenzie shifted his body until he could lean against a wall and face Jin. "Are you all right?" he asked.

"Yes."

113

"What did Fletcher do? Did he hurt you?"

"It felt like he was going to tear my arm off after I tripped him. When he brought me here, the other one – Bauer – got angry. He said if anyone had seen Fletcher with me, they might have gone to the police. Fletcher told him the police wouldn't care about a Chinese boy. You and I were a gang that stole their things, he said. If they kept me, you would be the only one who would come to find me."

"I guess he was right about that. They didn't mention Albert?"

"Your friend? He was here?"

"Albert and I found stolen things in these crates. Valuables that belong to his parents." It seemed like a long time since he and Albert had looked through the boxes. "Albert was loaded down, but he left before anyone saw him. I found something that belongs to the Birdman but then the shoeshines spotted me. I would've been caught, except for you. Thanks, Jin."

"Yes. What is the man Brittner like? Do you think he will hurt you like Fletcher says?"

Mackenzie remembered what his father had told him about Mr. Brittner. "No. I'll talk to him when he gets back. He'll let us go."

"I hope that is soon," Jin said. "My uncle will be very unhappy that I am so late. There are many deliveries that I should be doing. The clothes in these bags will need to be washed again. The pole is broken. For all of this I will be blamed."

"But you were helping me. You didn't know what was going to happen."

"He will be angry with my father too. My uncle will say it was wrong for me to deliver laundry. It was wrong for my father to tell him that I could do it."

"You work hard, all the time."

"My uncle did not want me to do this. He will send my father and me back to Vancouver."

"He can't do that. The rest of your family is moving here."

"My uncle will do as he wishes." Jin rubbed his arm across his cheek. "If my family cannot be here together it will be my fault."

Jin was crying now. Feeling awkward, Mackenzie was silent for a few moments. Then, "I hope that doesn't happen, Jin," he said. "I want you and your whole family to stay here."

If only I'd told Mr. Brittner it was Albert's father's watch when I saw it, Mackenzie thought, none of this would have happened. He glanced again at his friend. And I should have gone back to help Jin instead of going to the hotel. But it's not too late. When Mr. Brittner comes, he might get angry at me for taking things. I'll just have to explain everything, then he'll let us go. He has to.

And if he doesn't, Mackenzie decided, I'm getting Jin and me out of here anyway.

FOR THE NEXT HOUR, Mackenzie listened to Fletcher and Bauer mutter to each other in the front of the store. He imagined the shoeshines sitting high in their chairs, watching out the window for Mr. Brittner's return. Sometimes one of the men jumped down from his perch and walked on creaking floorboards back and forth around the tables heaped with goods. Neither one ever looked into the storeroom. They've forgotten about us, Mackenzie decided.

He flexed his fingers and pushed against the rope binding his wrists. There was a bit of give. Fletcher was no cowboy. If Mackenzie was a steer, he could easily break free of this knot. Jin's leather strap, he saw, was more tightly cinched against his skin.

A third voice rumbled through the store. Mr. Brittner! Mackenzie pushed himself straight back against the wall. "It won't be long now, Jin."

Soon they heard the three men marching toward them and a moment later Mr. Brittner filled the doorway.

"It's the Davis kid," the storekeeper said, rubbing the bumps on his head and stepping into the store-room. "How stupid can you get, tying him up in here?"

"That was Fletcher's idea." Bauer followed Mr. Brittner. "He didn't want the kid running to the cop-pers." The shoeshine nodded at the crates. "Now he's seen too much."

"And he stole from us," Fletcher said, slapping his fist into his palm.

Mr. Brittner walked to one of the boxes. Kicking at the papers strewn on the floor, he crossed his arms over his chest and glared at Mackenzie.

"You did this?" he snarled. "After I'd given you what you wanted for free, you came back and turned thief?"

"I can explain," Mackenzie said. "We were looking for Mr. Crawley's pocket watch. I asked you about it. Remember? I thought I recognized it. Then I found out it really was his. I wanted to get it back before it got sold by mistake."

"So you broke in here and pawed through all these crates. A hungry bear couldn't have made a worse mess. And it wasn't just that watch you took. You had something with you when Fletcher chased you out of here."

"He had it wrapped in that towel," Fletcher said. "I know what it was."

"It was a model of Mr. Martin's aeroplane," Mackenzie said. "It went missing from his hotel room. I took it back."

"He's been a regular little Robin Hood," Bauer said.

"How long was he gone before he came back for the Chinese kid?" Mr. Brittner asked.

"Five minutes," Fletcher said. "No more."

The storekeeper nodded. "No bobbies snooping around here yet. But this means a change in our plans. We won't have much time."

"Mr. Brittner," Mackenzie said, "you have to let us go! I didn't come here to steal anything. I just wanted to find those things and return them." He shot a glance at Bauer, who crossed his arms and glared back. "It's getting late. Our parents won't know where we are."

Fletcher pulled a rag from the pocket of his apron and snapped it near Mackenzie's face. Startled, Mackenzie cringed.

The shoeshine grinned. "Yappy little pup, isn't he? Like a stray mongrel. I'll stuff this in his mouth to shut him up."

"No," Mr. Brittner said. "We've got to treat him better than that." He winked at Bauer. "Don't you know who his father is? Get him up. The other one, too. They've been there long enough. Follow me." Mr. Brittner headed into the store.

Mackenzie raised his bound hands and Bauer tugged him to his feet. Jin sprang up and stumbled into Mackenzie before catching his balance.

He's going to let us go. Through the front door, even, Mackenzie thought. It'll be a quick run up the hill for me. Mother won't have had time to get really worried.

But the storekeeper had a different intention and led them to a door Mackenzie hadn't seen before. Opening it, Brittner stepped aside. Bauer shoved Mackenzie to the brink of a set of stairs that led down into a pit so black Mackenzie couldn't see anything below the first few steps. Stale, musty air gushed from the hole.

"Take them down," Mr. Brittner said. "There's a lantern there somewhere. Give them a bit of light."

Mackenzie felt Bauer push him over the edge of the first step. "But, Mr Brittner!" he cried.

"Quiet!" A meaty hand fell onto Mackenzie's shoulder and pinched his skin. "You keep your mouth shut and you'll be out of there pronto." Mr. Brittner's voice softened. "It's too dangerous for you up here right now."

Mackenzie's foot slid onto the second step. "Pick up your feet," Bauer muttered, "or I'll let go and watch you break your neck on the way to the bottom."

"Get the little Chinaman down there, too," Mr. Brittner said. "And, here, take this rope for their feet. I don't want them trying to scuttle off when we're not looking."

His hopes dashed, Mackenzie staggered down the remaining stairs.

SITTING ON THE DIRT FLOOR with his feet bound in front of him and his back against a crumbling dirt wall, Mackenzie eyed his friend. If they were kept in the basement much longer, things could get a lot worse for Jin than for him. Mackenzie had a mother and a father and a sister to go home to, and no one threatening to send them two thousand miles away to Vancouver.

"Are you worried about your father and your uncle?" he asked.

Jin nodded.

"It's getting late," Mackenzie said, "probably suppertime at least. It'll start to get dark soon." He nodded toward the stairs. "They're awfully quiet up there. I wish I could hear what they're talking about. Do you want to know how all this began, Jin? It's really stupid. We started raising flies in manure. Can you think of anything more foolish? Breeding flies. It was Albert's idea, of course," he began.

Mackenzie finished his tale a few minutes later. "And after I escaped from that man at the Flanagan Hotel," he said, "I came right here. By then you were already tied up. You know the rest. I'm sorry."

"Where did your friend Albert run to?" Jin asked. "Why has he not come back for you?"

"I've been wondering that too," Mackenzie said. "I think he doesn't know that I was caught."

"But you came here together. Would he not want to see you again, to talk about what happened?"

"Yes, except he probably went right to his father's office to show him that he'd found their stolen things. Then, if his father wasn't too busy, they'd go home to tell his mother. It was really important to Albert for his parents to see that everything was back. And that he was the one who got them."

"How could he just forget about you?" Jin asked. "It seems to me Albert thinks too much about himself."

"I suppose he does. I still like him. We have a lot of fun together. I never know what scheme he'll come up with next."

"But it sounds like you do most of the work."

"Yep!" Mackenzie laughed. "That's how it is sometimes." But breaking into Brittner's was different, Mackenzie thought. Albert did all of the hard stuff. I just got caught. "His family might have to move, too," he said, "like yours. I don't want to lose either of you as friends."

Overhead, three pairs of boots scuffed across the floor toward the back of the building. As the men passed the open doorway, Mackenzie heard Mr. Brittner talking. "Bauer, you get over to Durham's," he said. "Rent a good wagon and a strong team. Don't skimp on it, we can't have any breakdowns. Say we're going out to pick up an estate and we'll be gone a couple of days. Pay them what they want. Take these bills. That should be enough."

"What about me?" Fletcher asked.

"You stay here. Get everything wrapped up and back in the boxes. And keep an eye on our guests. Make sure they're comfortable." The men laughed. "I'm going to clean out my account at the bank. As soon as Bauer gets back, start loading the crates. We'll take what we can and leave the rest."

The footsteps continued into the storeroom. Mackenzie heard the back door open, then slap shut. One of the men – it must be Fletcher – walked to the front of the store. From the sound of his footsteps over the next few minutes, Mackenzie decided the shoeshine was circling from table to table around the shop.

They're going to make their getaway, Mackenzie thought. Hightail it out of town with all the loot they can carry. Will they ever let us go?

"They are going to keep us tied up here," Jin said, as if answering Mackenzie's question. "They know if they release us we will tell on them."

At the sound of a foot striking the top step both boys grew silent. They watched as two boots and a pair of black dress trousers descended into their dim light. Fletcher. For a moment Mackenzie couldn't figure out how he'd changed. Fletcher had swapped his stained shoeshine clothes for some fancy ones, the black pants and an unbuttoned black suit jacket. Grinning, he stepped onto the dirt floor.

"Not as smart as you thought you were, eh, boys? Probably wishing you'd never tangled with the likes of me. I told you you'd be sorry, didn't I?"

The arms of the jacket were too long. Fletcher tugged at them to pull the ends away from his hands.

He took those clothes from the hooks upstairs, Mackenzie decided. There must be lots of things they're leaving behind.

"You're a pitiful younker," Fletcher said to Mackenzie. "Keeping friends with a Chinaman."

"He's a better friend than you'd be," Mackenzie said. "He doesn't steal all the time. Or hurt people."

"Oh! Did I hurt you? Poor boy! You just be glad I didn't have this when the Chinaman smacked me with that bag." Fletcher slowly lifted the bottom of his jacket to reveal the molded rubber handle of a revolver stuck into his belt.

"That got your attention, didn't it?" Fletcher said,

releasing the jacket to fall over the gun. "Don't think I won't use it, either. Couple of weasels like you." He patted his jacket. "Brittner's so busy he's not going to notice what goes on down here."

Mackenzie had stopped breathing. His eyes were fixed on where the revolver had disappeared beneath Fletcher's jacket.

The shoeshine sneered. "Cat got your tongues, I see. You'll do well to keep it that way." He swung around and started up the stairs. "I'll be back," he said. "I'm not finished with you two yet."

Mackenzie let out his breath. That does it, he decided. "Jin," he whispered, "we're leaving."

MACKENZIE WAITED until he heard Fletcher's footsteps at the front of the store. Then he flattened himself on the dirt floor and grabbed his leg.

"What are you doing?" Jin asked.

"Cutting us free," Mackenzie said, inching his fingers up his pant leg. "I was wrong about Mr. Brittner. He's not the kind person he pretends to be." Mackenzie snagged his knife as it fell from his pocket and struggled to sit upright against the wall again. Unfolding the blade with his fingertips, he held out the knife to Jin.

"Do mine first," he said.

Jin set the knife on a loop of Mackenzie's rope and began sawing the blade back and forth.

"Hold your hands steady," Jin said. "I do not want to poke you."

"You won't. Do you see the crowd watching you?"

Jin swivelled to peer around the basement. "Where?"

Mackenzie nodded toward a darkened wall. "Look closely," he said. "The lamplight is reflected in their eyes."

"Yes," Jin said. "There's a pair. And another. Now I see them. It is like when the first stars come out at night. What are they?"

"Salamanders. They must have tunnels coming out all over that wall. That's good."

"Why?"

"It means that there won't be any snakes in here. There's just one or the other. At least that's what my mother says. And she would know. She hates snakes."

"Does she? Not my mother. She will tell you that seeing a snake is a good sign. A snake is wise and beautiful and you should never harm her." Jin grabbed Mackenzie's wrist and pressed the knife more firmly on the rope.

"I hope seeing salamanders is a good sign, too," Mackenzie said. "You're almost through."

Moments later, Mackenzie tore away the rope and massaged his wrists. "Now you," he said. Then, "Shh!"

Fletcher approached the open basement door. Muttering to himself, he passed into the storeroom.

"He's finally doing what Mr. Brittner told him to,"

Mackenzie whispered, "repacking the crates. The other two must be coming back soon."

"Cut your feet free."

"I will, but first your hands."

"No. Do your feet and then get out of here."

"What? I'm not going without you."

"Yes. It will take too long, Mackenzie. Your knife will not even cut through this tough leather. If you go now you can race to the station and bring back the police. They will catch these men before they can get away."

"And leave you here?" Mackenzie sat back and stared at his friend. "That isn't safe, Jin. If Fletcher finds you alone, he might..."

"Hurry! Cut the rope on your feet. Then listen for when Fletcher goes to the front of the store again. He left the key in the back door, did you see? This time you are not carrying anything. Even if he spots you, you will outrun him."

Mackenzie tested the blade against the rope binding his feet. A half-dozen tiny strands split apart. Jin's right, he thought. I'll be gone only five or six minutes. If I find an officer on patrol, even less. Fletcher wouldn't really hurt Jin. Mackenzie pushed down hard and watched the blade slice through the rope. "He won't hurt him," he told himself, "because he won't have time."

Soon the second loop of rope lay in the dirt. Mackenzie waited impatiently beside Jin, listening to Fletcher toss objects into the crates. A few pieces shattered, raising a curse from the shoeshine. He doesn't care if things break or not, Mackenzie thought. Maybe not even a person.

Fletcher's footsteps ground slowly overhead again, this time toward the storefront. Mackenzie stood up and slipped the knife into his pocket.

Looking down at Jin, he asked, "Are you sure?"

Jin nodded and lowered his head as if he was afraid he might change his mind.

Carefully listening for any sound from Fletcher, Mackenzie crept up the stairs and crouched on the top step. For the moment he knew he could not be seen by either Jin or Fletcher. He prepared to spring.

THE BOOTS CAME DOWN the stairs so quietly they were almost at the bottom before Jin looked up, baffled.

"Why are you here?" he asked.

"I couldn't do it," Mackenzie whispered.

"You didn't escape? Why? Go now!"

"I can't leave you here alone, Jin. I did it once and I know it was wrong. I'm not going to abandon you again."

"Where have you been?"

"Nowhere. I was just sitting at the top of the stairs. I came back down because I heard a wagon stopping in the alley. It must be Bauer back." Mackenzie slid down beside Jin.

"What if Fletcher comes down here again? He'll see you're not tied up."

"Fletcher's too stupid," Mackenzie said, loosely coiling the ropes around his ankles and wrists. "This time, whatever happens is going to happen to both of us."

"You should have got away," Jin said quietly.

WHEN BAUER RAPPED on the back door, Fletcher immediately scurried from the front to open it.

"Where did you get those things you're wearing?" Bauer asked. "You look like some greenhorn dude."

"They're mine. I found them. Remember? In that house last week."

"Brittner won't be happy to see you wearing them."

"He won't care. He's leaving them behind anyway. That's not all."

"I know where you found that, too. Put it back. We've got no need of one of those."

"Nope. I'm keeping it."

Bauer swore. Then, "We've got to get to work. Help me with the crates."

"Those kids wrecked everything," Fletcher complained. "We had a perfect set-up and now we have to vamoose."

"Don't get yourself worked into a knot," Bauer said. "We were going to have to move soon anyway. The old man'll fix us up somewhere else. You'll see. Could be we'll go back stateside. I wouldn't mind that. All he needs is an empty store and a couple of shoeshine chairs. Lift!"

For the next few minutes the men grunted, cursed

and plodded with heavy footsteps across the store-room.

"Soon they will leave," Jin said.

"Yes. They might not even come down," Mackenzie said. "They're in such a big rush."

Brittner's voice boomed through the store. "Time to get out of here, boys! The coppers'll be out looking for those kids. We don't want to be around for that. Leave the rest. Bauer, you get behind the reins. Where's Fletcher?"

The shoeshine was near the bottom of the steps. He jumped to the floor, lifted up the flap of his jacket and pulled the gun from under his belt.

"They won't even hear this upstairs," he muttered, slowly pointing the gun around the basement walls.

Squeezing his arms and legs together, Mackenzie hoped Fletcher didn't look too closely at the ropes.

"Brittner's going to thank me when I tell him about this," Fletcher said. "We won't have to worry about you two blabbing anything." The shoeshine lowered the gun and stepped toward Jin.

I have to yell, Mackenzie decided. Mr. Brittner wouldn't want him to do this.

But it was Bauer's voice that caught his partner's attention.

"Fletcher! Are you down there? Don't be a fool. Get up here!"

"I can come back," Fletcher said, "anytime I please. Wait and see if I don't." Replacing the handgun, he dropped the jacket flap, turned around and took the stairs two at a time.

"Leave those two be," Mr. Brittner growled. "What's that under your jacket? Get rid of it. I don't mind you being light-fingered with my clothes, but you're not taking that thing anywhere."

Fletcher said something in a whining voice that Mackenzie didn't catch.

"Grab that shovel and axe," the storekeeper said, "and throw them in the wagon. They're going to come in handy."

Again Mackenzie found himself holding his breath. He listened for any more sounds of the men. Ten seconds. Twenty seconds. Thirty. He flopped back against the wall and didn't even notice the avalanche of pebbly dirt that streamed down the back of his shirt.

"They're gone," he said. "We did it." Pushing himself up, he added, "Now let me see that leather."

When his arms and legs were free, Jin lifted the lantern, turned up the wick, and followed Mackenzie up the stairs. As they stepped onto the main floor the wavering light cast trembling shadows toward the shop and hurried the boys into the storeroom. Mackenzie snapped on the light bulb.

"My bags," Jin said. "I must get them back to the laundry."

"You won't be able to take them both. Your pole is broken, remember? I'll carry one for you. Then I'll run home. Ow!" Jin had pinched Mackenzie's arm. "Why did you do that?"

Jin pointed to the door and the two of them watched it swing open. Oh no, Mackenzie thought. Fletcher didn't leave.

When the door opened fully, a burly policeman stepped into the room. Taking in the empty shelves and knocked-over boxes, the officer folded his arms across his chest.

"I thought I heard voices in here," he said. "It seemed a strange time for a light to be on in Mr. Brittner's store. What exactly are you lads up to at this hour?"

"I can explain," Mackenzie said. "Mr. Brittner sells things that have been stolen. This is where he keeps them."

"Stolen items? Here?" The officer examined the room. "I don't see much that matches that description. What I see are two boys caught red-handed where they've no business being. I expect that it's Mr. Brittner who can tell us what's gone missing, not the likes of you."

The officer stopped talking and peered at Mackenzie. "Wait a minute," he said. "Are you the Davis boy?"

Mackenzie nodded.

"You have half the police force out looking for you. Your mother's fit to be tied. What in tarnation are you doing hiding in here?"

"I'm not hiding. Mr. Brittner and the shoeshines tied us up. We just cut ourselves free, Jin and I."

The officer frowned and swung his gaze to Jin as if he hadn't noticed him before. "Who are you?" he asked.

"Jin."

"Mr. Lee is his uncle," Mackenzie interjected. "Jin works at the laundry."

"Mr. Lee?" the officer asked. "I know Mr. Lee. He does my shirts. I certainly don't know what to think of your story, lads. All I was told was that we had one missing boy. I'm going to take you to the station." He pointed at Mackenzie. "Your father's already there. Then I'll go get Mr. Lee. He must be worried sick as well."

Mackenzie cringed at the thought of his father waiting at the police station and his mother alone with Nellie at home. They were going to be really angry. And he deserved it. Even Mr. Lee and Jin's father will be upset with me, he told himself.

THE ROOM WAS SMALLER than Mackenzie's bedroom and half the space was taken up by a wooden desk behind which Sergeant Devereux wrote carefully on a pad of paper. Across from him, Mackenzie and his father sat side by side on hard wooden chairs. Mackenzie held his hand over his mouth and yawned. It felt like he'd been sitting in this room for hours. He wasn't looking forward to what his mother was going to say, but he was so tired he wanted nothing more than to go home.

Behind Sergeant Devereux a window looked into a hallway and a steady stream of blue-uniformed police officers coming and going from a row of doorways. Not long after Mackenzie and his father had been placed in the room, he had caught a glimpse of a frightened-looking Jin and his grim-faced father being taken down the hall. Later, Albert and his father had arrived. Clenching the blue jewellery bag in his fist, Albert had spotted Mackenzie and grinned at him through the window while an officer directed him and his father through one of the doors."

"Everything's checking out, Ted," the sergeant said, capping his pen and setting it on the desk. "Brittner's bank account is cleaned out. One of his boys rented a rig. The few things we've been able to get a look at in that back room seem to match items that have been stolen over the past few months." He shook his head. "I don't know how we missed seeing this earlier. It was the shoeshines, right? They'd get their customers talking about themselves. If they heard anything promising, those folks would be targets for their thievery. Like Lozar and his family sleeping in a tent. Or Mr. Crawley taking his wife's jewellery out of his office safe and leaving it unprotected at home."

Mr. Martin, Mackenzie thought, must have told the shoeshines about the silver model he kept in his hotel room. He felt his eyes closing as he leaned against his father's arm. Did the Birdman get his model back? he wondered.

"So those two were the robbers," Mackenzie's father said. "Fletcher and Bauer. And they gave everything to

Brittner who kept the stolen things out of sight in the back room. He had me fooled completely." Putting his arm around his son, he added, "Unfortunately, Mackenzie believed me and ended up trusting Brittner more than he deserved."

Mackenzie opened his eyes. "Albert sure didn't," he said. "He figured out what Mr. Brittner was doing. When we snuck in and found those things, he knew they'd been stolen."

"It was about then, if not sooner, that you boys should have told me," Mackenzie's father said. "We could have gone right to Sergeant Devereux."

"I'm sorry," Mackenzie said. "We didn't think we'd get caught." In his mind, he saw himself jumping from Mr. Brittner's back door, staggering, catching his balance, then racing down the lane with Fletcher at his heels. "Jin saved me," he said. "He could have just stood there. I feel bad that Fletcher was so mean to him." Suddenly, Mackenzie remembered what Albert had said about the police.

"Did you used to think that it was the Chinese people who were stealing from houses?" he asked the sergeant.

"Which Chinese people?"

"The ones who deliver laundry, like Jin. Albert told me the police thought they looked in people's houses when they brought their laundry and watched for things to steal."

"What an imagination!" the sergeant said, chuckling.

"No, I can assure you we never suspected your friend Jin and Mr. Lee in these robberies."

"Where do you think Brittner and his boys have gone?" Mackenzie's father asked.

"That's anyone's guess," Sergeant Devereux said. "The way they were packed up, I figure they were getting ready to vamoose soon anyway. They seem to have gotten out of town without anyone noticing." He pulled a watch from his coat pocket and snapped open the cover. "A couple of hours and it'll be light enough to get my men out looking. They won't get far loaded down like they are. We've already wired every station agent on every line going out of Saskatoon. They'll be watching for strangers matching their description coming through town or trying to board a train."

Mackenzie's eyes grew heavy again and his head lolled onto his chest. There was some sort of ruckus in the hallway but he was too tired to look up until he heard a voice cry, "I need to talk to the boy. His name's Mackenzie, I know that much. He's a young hero."

Mr. Martin stormed down the hall, pulling an officer in his wake. At each door he paused to peer through the small window into the room, then burst ahead. When he spotted Mackenzie, he cried, "Who's that? That's him, isn't it?"

"You can't go in there, sir," the officer said, reaching across the Birdman's chest. "The sergeant is conducting an interview."

"I won't hold him up. I just have to thank the lad."

Mr. Martin pushed the officer's arm aside and opened the door.

Turning in his chair, Sergeant Devereux glowered at the intruder. Mr. Martin ignored him.

"You're Mackenzie, am I right? Of course I am. By golly, boy, you've done me a great service. That model is more precious to me than my own aeroplane. This time next year I'll have a new flying machine, but that silver sculpture is one of a kind." Mr. Martin extended his hand across the table. Mackenzie stood up and shook it.

His father also got to his feet. "Ted Davis," he said.

"You're the lad's father? We've met before haven't we? You're with *The Daily Phoenix.*"

Sergeant Devereux scraped his chair across the floor and stood up. "We're finished for now, Ted," he said, picking up his pen and papers. "There's nothing more we need to do. You can get your boy home to bed. Good night." He nodded at the Birdman. "Mr. Martin," he said, and left the room.

"I'm glad Mackenzie was able to recover your model," his father said. "We're very proud of him. And we've been enjoying your performances."

"Thank you. They're nothing, really." He took a wallet from his suit pocket. "There's a reward for this. He certainly deserves it."

"That's not necessary," Mackenzie's father said, shaking his head. "I expect it's been a big enough thrill just to meet you. Mackenzie would like nothing better than to be an aviator himself when he grows up – isn't that right, son?"

"Yes," Mackenzie said. Then, to Mr. Martin: "You're the best pilot I've ever seen."

"Well, thank you." Mr. Martin put away his wallet. "You're on your way, are you?"

"I'm walking Mackenzie home, then returning to *The Daily Phoenix* to write up some stories."

"Come over to my hotel for a few minutes on your way back, will you, Ted? I won't keep you, but there's something I'd like to discuss."

Mr. Martin thanked me! Mackenzie thought. With his mouth open in wonder and his eyes glued on the Birdman, Mackenzie felt wide awake. In the middle of the night he came to the police station to find me. What does he want to talk about? How can I convince Father to let me tag along and find out?

101 RANCH WILD WEST SHOW FILLS THREE TRAINS

Thrills and Dangers of Old West Re-lived

The Old West has disappeared from the prairies of North America as surely as the great herds of buffalo that used to roam over the wide ranges. Today, everywhere we look, the New West has taken hold with its booming cities and busy farms, its aeroplanes and motor cars and its telephones and moving pictures.

It is with great excitement that fairgoers have swarmed into the Exhibition grandstand to witness the return of the Old West in the form of the 101 Ranch Wild West Show. This entertainment was transported to our city on three entire trains directly from its last engagement in Chicago, U S of A. In the space of two hours audiences are witness to visions of reckless, daring cowboys, comely and intrepid cowgirls, old scouts and sun-darkened plainsmen, Mexican vaqueros, roving bands of Indians and a herd of genuine long-horned cattle taken from their range near Bliss, Oklahoma.

CHAPTER FIVE
Friday, August 9, 1912

"I DON'T KNOW THAT I SHOULD EVEN ALLOW YOU out of the house today, Mackenzie. I just want to lock you up and not let you go anywhere near downtown. It seems like you lose your good sense the moment you go across the river."

Mackenzie's mother took a deep breath. She was leaning against the stove, its steel side cooling now that breakfast had been prepared and the water in the kettle boiled. Her arms were crossed tightly over her chest and a scowl creased her forehead. At her feet, Nellie studied three cooking pots. Worried by the tone of her mother's voice, the baby looked up and then followed her mother's gaze across the room to where her brother was sitting.

"I'm sorry," Mackenzie said, dropping his eyes to the tabletop. He didn't want to say anything that would make her more upset. "I shouldn't have taken

Albert to Mr. Brittner's store. We thought that we could find his parents' things and be gone before anyone knew. We almost did it."

"Twice. Twice you went into that store when you should have gone directly to the police station. I expect you to know better."

"I do. Next time –"

"Next time! Mackenzie, surely there won't be a next time!"

"No. Do you want me to wash the dishes now?"

"I'm not finished." Mackenzie's mother released her arms and pointed at the little finger of one hand. "There's also the matter of taking my pie plate," she said. "*And*," touching the tip of her second finger, "not being truthful when I asked you about it. *And* putting that stinky mess in the box closet. *And* I haven't forgotten that knife cut in your boot which you seem to think I'm too blind to notice. Whatever you've been up to with that knife of yours, I'm sure it had nothing to do with whittling."

"But that's how we escaped, Jin and I. My knife was in my pocket. I used it to cut the ropes."

"That definitely was *not* why you were allowed to buy that knife – to escape from being tied up by thieves." Resting her hands on her hips, Mackenzie's mother went on. "It seems to me that any one of those is a perfectly good reason to have you stay here and miss the rest of the Exhibition. But all that pales in comparison to what your father has proposed for this afternoon. That's really why I want you locked up."

"I don't understand, Mother."

"He didn't tell you?"

"No. Father said to meet him after the grandstand show this afternoon. That's why I asked if you had anything for me to do before I went to the Exhibition."

"You and your father! I don't know who's worse. As a matter of fact, I do have a list. It starts with you cleaning out the box closet."

"Yes, Mother," Mackenzie said, trying to hide his grin. "And how about Nellie? Should I wash her some carrots?"

MACKENZIE STARED at the hand-printed "CLOSED" sign tacked to the front of the laundry. He couldn't remember a time when the door to Mr. Lee's shop hadn't opened to its jangling bell.

Where are they? Why isn't it open? Why didn't Mr. Lee go with Jin and his father to the police station last night? Was Mr. Lee really angry with them? Mackenzie's mind raced. Maybe Mr. Lee already has closed the laundry. Jin and his father have been sent away. They left on the early train to Vancouver. I'm not going to see him again, Mackenzie decided.

What about Father's shirts? he wondered. How will I get them back? Fingering the red ticket in his trousers pocket, Mackenzie went back across the bridge, climbed the hill to Broadway Avenue and followed the riverbank north.

When he reached Albert's yard, Mackenzie took the sidewalk to the back of the house. He turned the knob fastened to the centre of the door and heard the crank grind against the bell inside. Stepping back, he was surprised to see Madame La Claire come out. Without looking at Mackenzie, the fortune teller walked down the stairs and around the corner of the house.

A moment later Albert stuck his head out. "I thought that might be you," he said, eyeing Mackenzie. "Are you really angry with me?"

"Where were you yesterday? Where did you go?"

"I didn't know anything had happened to you until last night when the coppers told us." Albert sat down on the stoop. Cradling his cast on his lap, he shifted over so there was room for Mackenzie. "I thought you skedaddled when I did."

"You didn't wonder when I didn't show up at the ABC?"

"Sure, I wondered, but I thought that you'd decided to go home or to the Fair."

"No."

"Why didn't you take off with me? You kept telling me they were coming."

"I found a model of a biplane that belonged to Mr. Martin. I knew it must be what had been stolen from his hotel room. By the time I got it out of the crate they were almost on me. I ran, but Fletcher was faster. You don't know about Jin, either, do you?"

"That's the Chinaman kid?"

"Yes." Mackenzie told Albert what had happened with him and Jin.

"Wow," Albert said. "If I'd known that, I would've come back. I really would have, Mack. You know that, don't you?"

"Sure."

"It sounds like Brittner could've really hurt you."

"I think he was bluffing. Fletcher would've, though. He really wanted to get back at Jin." How long will Jin and his father be on the train? he wondered. At least his family will be together again. "Jin and his father have been sent back to Vancouver."

"That's a better place for them. There are lots of Chinamen there."

"Quit saying things like that. Jin's my friend. I didn't want him to move. Anyway, why did you tell me that story about the police thinking the Chinese laundry boys were helping thieves? I asked Sergeant Devereux. He said it wasn't true."

Albert shrugged. "That's what I heard the coppers say. I didn't make it up."

"I'm going to miss him," Mackenzie said. "What did your parents say when they saw their things?"

"They were amazed. My mother had given up hope of ever getting them back. That's not all," Albert said. "I just found out we're not moving."

"Your father said so? That's great, Albert."

"He didn't say so. Madame La Claire did."

"Albert! What are you talking about! Has your father told you anything?"

"No, not since he said that St. Louis couldn't come up with the money. But he's not going to his office this afternoon or tonight. He's taking my mother and me to the Exhibition."

"So he's not expecting any more telegrams? That's almost like telling you the deal's off. Your Madame La Claire was wrong. The person who found the jewellery isn't taking a big trip. Her predictions aren't so good after all." Did Albert actually talk to the fortune teller? Mackenzie wondered. He remembered what he'd heard Madame La Claire tell Albert on Broadway Avenue. She'd made it sound like it would take hours to read his palm.

"Did she really tell you that?"

"Of course!"

"Albert, you have so many stories I never know when to believe you."

There was something else the fortune teller said on Broadway, too. "What did she mean by that illusion stuff?" Mackenzie asked. "That illusions hide the truth?"

"Like Brittner," Albert said. "You were convinced he was a nice man, but look what he did to you. Shoot! I should've asked her where Brittner was, too."

"She wouldn't know."

"My father says that gang'll be well on their way to the u.s. border by now," Albert said. "If they got on a train, they'll be across already. Brittner'll find some boom town in Colorado or Wyoming and they'll carry on their thieving ways. He won't show his face around here again, that's for sure."

"You're probably right," Mackenzie said. "Albert, I cleaned out the box closet."

"No! What did you do that for? Tomorrow's the contest."

"I had to tell my parents. My mother wanted to know everything. She made me get rid of the manure and her pie plate."

"You threw it all out?"

"Yes. Don't ask me any more. It was disgusting. I don't want to talk about it."

"Were there many flies? Do you think that we might have won?"

"Albert, it was a really stupid idea."

Sighing, Albert muttered, "One more day, that's all we needed."

"Well, it's too late now." Mackenzie stood up. "I have a few more things I have to do for my mother."

"Are you going to the grandstand later?"

"What do you think? It's the last Wild West Show. And the last flight for the Birdman. Of course I'll be there."

AN INDIAN FAMILY entered the field, the women and children walking slowly beside men on horseback who wore beaded leather jackets and feathered headdresses. A few of the women carried babies in pouches strapped to their backs. Some of the children held the leads of other horses that dragged the long poles of travois loaded with tanned hides and blankets and resting toddlers. When the group stopped near the front of the grandstand, the men slid off their mounts. The older children lifted the younger ones from the travois while their mothers pulled off bags and pieces of firewood. As if guided by the voice of the announcer – the same one who had told about Lulu Carr and Blue Belle – the family began to set up their camp.

Mackenzie studied the sky over the bleachers. The Birdman had taken his aeroplane to a safe place away from the Exhibition. When he'd landed yesterday, a hundred people had swarmed onto the grass in front of him and forced him to steer off course. Two of the struts that held the wings together had been bent when the wheels struck rough ground. Has the mechanic fixed the posts? Mackenzie wondered. When will the Birdman show up? Will he fly low across the prairie this time or storm over the midway?

The announcer's voice brought him back to the Wild West Show. The Indian family was gone, replaced by two canvas-covered wagons, each pulled by a team of four oxen. In a solemn tone, the announcer warned the audience that for many years

Indians and pioneers had fought each other in the American west. The people peering from inside the wagons were pretending to be early settlers. The wagons halted and the families got down and began to lift off their goods. Suddenly fierce cries and rifle shots split the air. A dozen men pretending to be Indian warriors galloped onto the field. Decorated with face paint, wearing moccasins and breechcloths and holding aloft bows and rifles, the riders guided their ponies around the wagons and traded shots with the pioneers. One by one the guns fell silent as settlers and Indians slumped forward in death.

That's not what happened in Canada, Mackenzie thought. Father says more Indians helped pioneers than ever hurt them.

While the audience around him murmured, the actors sprang back to life, picked up everything that had fallen to the ground and scrambled off the field.

After time for a quick change in costumes, twelve Mexican riders appeared and began to circle the field atop matching white horses. Dwarfed by their huge straw sombreros, the vaqueros wore black vests over billowing white shirts. The smiling horsemen danced swirling lassos in unison from one side of their mounts to the other and raised cheers and applause for their feat.

Mackenzie spotted Albert climbing toward him. Cradling a bag of popcorn in his sling, Albert waved the telescope in his free hand. Mackenzie smiled. Now he had everything he needed to enjoy the final performance.

THE BIRDMAN was nowhere in sight. On his first swing over the bleachers, minutes before, Mr. Martin's aeroplane had seemed to be not much higher that the top of the grandstand. With a wave to the crowd, he had set off on a huge figure eight that didn't end until he was a mile away at the river. Then he sailed back to the fairgrounds. Only when he flew right overhead for a second time did Mackenzie understand that the Birdman was steadily gaining altitude.

"He's going to climb as high as he can," Mackenzie told Albert. "Over a mile. Can you see anything?"

"It looks like a speck of dirt on the lens," Albert said as he handed over the telescope and dug in his pocket for a crumpled bag of peanuts.

Mackenzie put the telescope to one eye and tracked the biplane.

The people around the boys grew restless. "Is this all we get for our money?" a man asked.

"He might make history," another one said, "if he breaks the record."

LIKE A HAWK diving out of the blue to snatch a gopher, the aeroplane plunged silently toward the earth. A speck became a point, a point a dot, a dot a fly, the fly grew stiff double wings that sheltered a pilot who pulled on his controls and ended the fall a thousand feet above the ground. As the crowd applauded, Mr. Martin turned his craft into a colossal corkscrew that circled lower and lower between the grandstand and the midway. On one pass over the rides he suddenly shut off the engine and dipped the nose of the aeroplane. As if it were on a giant slide, the biplane swept to the earth, causing a few faint-hearted to scream and many to catch their breath. This time he didn't pull up until, moments before he was sure to crash, he levelled the craft, let the wheels touch the ground and coasted to a stop.

A huge wave of applause burst from the grandstand and continued while Mr. Shannon walked to the biplane and spoke with Mr. Martin. The mechanic turned to the bleachers and raised both palms. For a moment he held up five fingers on his right hand and his thumb on the left. Then he dropped his left hand and showed four fingers on his right.

"That's the signal!" the announcer cried from his platform near the front seats. "Mr. Martin reports that he has set a new altitude record. Six thousand four hundred feet!" Cheers exploded from the stands as Mr. Shannon stepped to the front of the craft, grasped one tip of the propeller and pulled the engine into life. The aeroplane shot across the field and rose smoothly over the peaked white tents.

"That's it," Mackenzie said. "That was his last flight."

"Where's he off to in his aeroplane?" Albert asked.

"His flatcar's on a Canadian Northern siding not far from here. That's where he started from on Monday. He'll land there and he and the mechanic will take the aeroplane apart and pack it in their crates again. He leaves for Chicago tonight."

The boys stood up. All around them, people were shuffling from the plank seats and making their slow way down the stairs. Mackenzie held out the telescope.

"No," Albert said, "you keep it for awhile. It's half yours anyway." He reached his foot down to the next seat. "I'm not waiting for these turtles." Catching his balance, Albert stretched to touch the plank below that. Mackenzie followed. Already a small gang of boys scurried like squirrels after a picnic over the planks and beneath the seats gathering the leftover trash before the final grandstand performances that evening.

On the other side of the tents, hidden from the fair-goers, the Wild West Show performers were busy packing up costumes and riding gear. When their kits were complete, the men and women joined a line that took them to a trail boss who handed each of them a pay packet.

At the entrance gate, the boys found people standing about in twos and threes watching for stragglers, chatting with friends or gathering together children before they boarded the train to downtown or found their buggy in a nearby pasture. Albert quickly spotted his parents and joined them as they walked to their waiting motor car.

Mackenzie's father stood near the gate, speaking to one after another of the fairgoers. After tipping his hat to the man selling tickets, he left the grounds and waved for Mackenzie to follow.

"Your mother's got you dressed up, I see," Mackenzie's father said. "Even your Sunday shoes. We have a distance to walk. I hope your feet won't get too sore in them."

"They won't. How far are we going?"

"About a mile, straight south. What's that you've got?"

"Albert's telescope. He said I could borrow it." Mackenzie slipped the tube into his trousers pocket.

"What did your mother say about this?" his father asked.

"Nothing."

"She's being good about it. She was dead set against this proposition, I can tell you. It took a lot of convincing. Even when she finally gave in, she couldn't bring herself to come along. That's why she stayed home with Nellie."

"Why can't you tell me what we're doing?"

"I can now. It had to be a secret. If I'd let you know this morning, you wouldn't have been able to tell anyone all day. You see, Mr. Martin is determined to reward you for finding that precious model of his. When he learned about your interest in flying, he offered to take you up."

"In the air?" Mackenzie grabbed his father's sleeve. "I'm going to fly?"

"Only if you're sure that's what you want to do."

"Snap! Father, of course that's what I want to do."

Mackenzie's father smiled. "I thought you would."

Mackenzie released his hand. "Aren't we going the wrong way? I thought he was landing by the tracks."

"Mr. Martin wanted to keep this quiet. He didn't want it turning into a circus with people crowding around to watch. On one of his flights he found a flat spot near the river. That's where we're meeting him." Mackenzie's father pulled a watch from his pocket. "And we'd better hustle a bit. We don't want to keep him waiting." Hurrying to stay even with his father, Mackenzie had to stop himself from skipping like a young child. For the next quarter mile he peppered his father with questions. "Did Mr. Martin show you his model? What else did he tell you about it? How did you convince Mother? Where will we fly?"

Finally he was content just to quietly follow a deeply rutted trail that led in and out of gullies and around bluffs of trees. The greyish green leaves of sage plants hugging the earth between the ruts filled the air with a soothing scent. Patches of tiny yellow flowers hung from thin stems that grew no higher than Mackenzie's boot. His mother would know what they were called.

"Thousands of wagons have passed by here and dug these tracks," Mackenzie's father said, pointing to the grooves cut into the earth. "That's a lot of settlers."

"Why did they all come *this* way?"

"Before they laid down the train tracks, this was a main route going north and south. It's how people travelled between here and Moose Jaw and even the States. Down near the elbow in the river, it meets the old Métis cart trail that ran from Winnipeg to Edmonton. The old-timers around here would know lots of local paths coming off of it, too."

"What about Mr. Brittner? Do you think this is where he went?"

"Oh, that Mr. Brittner! I shiver to think what I put you through because I gave you such wrong advice about the man. It's a mystery where he's gotten to. A whole day's gone by and Sergeant Devereux hasn't had so much as a sighting."

Somewhere behind them a harness bell tinkled. Mackenzie and his father turned to see a horse and buggy coming their way. A man and a boy shared the wagon seat and two horses, their reins tied to the buggy, followed behind. Mackenzie's father cupped his hand over his eyes. "I forgot," he said. "This trail goes past the Whitecap Reserve. Those two are probably on their way home."

A few minutes later the buggy pulled alongside. Mackenzie recognized the man wearing the feathered stetson and the boy with the grey tweed cap pulled low on his forehead.

"Are you men lost?" the man asked, smiling. "You've got a lot of walking to do before you get to anywhere around here."

"I was told there's a big slough with a flat piece of land close by. That's where we're going."

"You've got quite a walk ahead of you," the man said. "You'd better jump in the back. Save yourself some shoe leather."

Pulling on the reins, the boy spoke softly to the horse and the buggy stopped.

"Sit anywhere you like," the man said. "You won't hurt anything."

When they climbed onto the bed of the buggy, Mackenzie found some wooden boxes, two saddles, a grey canvas bag and a collection of bridles, reins, and traces thrown into a corner. He and his father settled onto a pile of blankets as the boy clicked his tongue and the horse ambled off. Soon they were jiggling in a kind of jerky rhythm as the wagon's wheels dropped into holes and rubbed against the sides of the ancient ruts.

"Thanks for doing this," Mackenzie's father called.

Shifting in his seat so he could see toward the back, the man nodded.

"I'm Ted Davis. This is my son, Mackenzie."

"It's our pleasure. My name is Joseph Bear. This is Junior."

"Have you been at the Exhibition?" Mackenzie's father asked.

"We were in it," Joseph Bear said, smiling. "Junior and I were extras for the Wild West Show."

"I saw you at the harness shop getting your stuff

ready," Mackenzie said. "What did you do in the show?"

"Any time there were Indians, I was there," Junior said, looking over his shoulder. "I even got to shoot blanks at the wagons."

"Junior is a real good trick rider," Joseph Bear said. "He learned from his grandfather."

"Not you?" Mackenzie's father asked, looking at the things spread over the bottom of the wagon. "You must know a lot about horses."

"Raised them all my life but I'm no fancy rider." Joseph Bear laughed. "Slow and easy, that's good enough for me."

"You weren't one of the men attacking the wagon?" Mackenzie asked.

" No. The only wagon I attack is the chuckwagon."

"He does not ride fast," Junior said, "but he keeps everyone's gear fixed so they can."

"Are other extras in the Wild West Show from around here?" Mackenzie's father asked.

"Most of those people travel with the show. They hire a few locals to make it look like there are lots of cowboys and Indians. Our boys and their friends from off the reserve spend their days on a horse anyway, chasing steers and lassoing calves. If someone wants to pay them to do it, they're more than happy to oblige."

"Where are they?"

"They'll be coming along." Joseph chuckled.

"Some of them were waiting to get their wages so they could spend them at the midway."

Pulling on the reins and clicking his tongue, Junior guided the horse off the trail. Chattering red-winged blackbirds rose from a ring of cattails bordering a green slough and swooped over the buggy.

"That's where you're heading," Joseph Bear said. "There's good duck hunting around here. But you two don't look dressed for hunting."

Mackenzie's father laughed. "No. No hunting for us. It's the flat meadow we're interested in. Did you see that fellow in his aeroplane at the Fair?"

"Yes!" Junior said. "One time he flew so low he scared the horses. I thought they were going to stampede."

"Well, that's who we're going to see. Mr. Martin's offered to give Mackenzie a short ride in the aeroplane."

Twisting around on the seat, the boy asked, "You're going to fly?"

"Yes."

"Can we watch?"

"I expect so," Mackenzie's father said. "I don't see why not."

Pushing himself to his feet, Mackenzie peered over Joseph and Junior and spotted the aeroplane. Mr. Martin and his mechanic stood beside the craft. A saddled horse, tied by his reins to a nearby bush, grazed on the dry grass. That's how Mr. Shannon got there.

Mackenzie felt his father tug on his pant leg. Trying to keep his eyes on the biplane, he dropped back down to the floor of the buggy.

"You know," his father said, "I wouldn't let you do this if I didn't think it was perfectly safe. But from the moment you step off the buggy you must listen carefully to everything Mr. Martin says. And do exactly as he asks."

"Yes, Father." Mackenzie could feel the buggy slowing down. He wanted badly to jump off and run to the aeroplane.

"There are many grown men who would refuse to leave the safety of the earth," his father continued. "If you change your mind, if you decide you don't want to fly, well, there's no shame in that. Mr. Martin will understand."

"I want to."

"And I'm proud you do."

As he scrambled over the side of the buggy, Mackenzie felt Albert's telescope in his pocket. He pulled it out and tossed it on a blanket. He dropped his hat beside it. As he walked toward the biplane, Mackenzie forced himself to take a couple of deep breaths, like his mother did when she was riding in a motor car. I'm going to fly, he told himself. I'm going to fly!

SOON MACKENZIE was huddled with Mr. Martin near the pilot's seat. Behind them, the mechanic snugged each nut with a wrench, drummed his fingers on the fabric tightly stretched over both wings and carefully tested each cable fastening the wings to the body of the craft. Pacing nearby, Mackenzie's father glanced at his son then quickly away, suddenly too nervous to look closely at the fragile machine. On a small rise about fifty yards off, Joseph and Junior watched from the seat of their buggy.

"Put these on," Mr. Martin said, handing Mackenzie a pair of goggles. "They're a spare set." Climbing onto the pilot's seat, Mr. Martin tapped the bottom wing to his left.

"You'll sit here," he said, "behind this strut. Mr. Shannon will hoist you up. Wrap your legs around and let your feet hang over the edge. That's right. Get a grip on the strut with your hands. Good lad. Now, whatever you do, don't let go of that post until we're back on the ground."

Mr. Martin pulled his goggles down and pointed behind him. A moment later the mechanic spun the propeller and the motor came alive, rocking the craft on its wheels. Five feet from the Birdman's back, the blades of the propeller quickly spun into a blur. The biplane jerked forward, its wheels bouncing over the grassy field.

Catching his father's eye, Mackenzie waved then clamped his hand back on the post. Soon the shocks came faster and faster, each one tossing Mackenzie lightly into the air and dropping him back onto the wing. Inches below his feet, the ground rushed past.

Mr. Martin, he remembered, had told his father this was one of the dangerous times in the flight of an aeroplane. Tightening his grip with both hands, Mackenzie clenched the pole between his legs. As if he could read Mackenzie's mind, the Birdman grinned and mouthed the words, "Good lad."

Suddenly the motor quietened. The wing began to hum, to vibrate beneath Mackenzie's seat. The wind whipping his face chilled. What's wrong? Mackenzie wondered. Then, lowering his eyes, his heart caught as the ground fell away, down, down, like he was at the top of a hill looking far below to the bottom. Am I flying? he wondered. Seconds later, he soared over a clump of twenty-foot trees, and there was no longer any doubt.

Below him a homestead cabin sat beside a neat square of yellow wheat. What looked like a black fly rose from the roof of the cabin, beating its strong black wings to lift itself onto a current of wind below the aeroplane. I'm higher than that crow, Mackenzie thought. I can see everything it sees.

The wind pushed against his body like a stormy blast, chilling his face and hands. This isn't so bad, Mackenzie thought. It's like when we sneak into the Arctic Ice wagon and rub our fingers over the frozen blocks.

Near the horizon in front of them, a train steamed toward the city. A funnel of grey and white cloud gushed from the locomotive and streamed back over the twenty cars behind. Then the Birdman turned the aeroplane into a wide loop that took it east away from the city. The train fell out of sight.

For the next few minutes, they roamed this way and that like a wide-winged eagle soaring over the endless prairie. Mackenzie wanted to memorize each new view so he could describe it to his parents and friends when he was back on the ground. But when he stared too long at one thing, he knew a dozen other sights were vanishing beneath the bottom wing.

One clump of poplar trees they cleared by what seemed like no more than a few feet. Looking down, Mackenzie was startled to see the faces of three men staring up at the sudden appearance of the aeroplane. In the few seconds they were visible to him, Mackenzie recognized the trio. He leaned over and yelled, "Mr. Martin!"

The Birdman didn't look his way. "Mr. Martin!" Mackenzie took one hand off the strut to wave. Immediately he felt like he was about to be blown off the wing. He clamped his hand back on the post. He would have to wait until they were back on the ground. But how, he wondered, would they ever find that bluff again?

The Birdman had already set his sights on the fair-grounds. In the distance, Mackenzie spotted the peaked white tents, the roof of the towering grandstand and the slowly turning circle of the Ferris wheel. Nearer to him, a cloud of grey dust drifted above a dozen horses and their riders cantering toward them on the pioneer trail. Less than two hundred yards away, his father and three others had gathered near the idle wagon.

The sound of the motor lightened. It's slowing down, Mackenzie thought. He and Mr. Martin were hurtling closer toward the earth and what the pilot said was the second most dangerous manoeuvre. Yesterday two struts had been damaged. Would they bend again? Or break? As the ground rushed up, impossibly close beneath his feet, the engine stopped entirely. For the next few seconds the only noise was the wind whistling across the wing fabric and the front sails snapping like the shoeshine's rag. Mackenzie wrapped himself around the wing strut and pinched his eyelids. A moment later, the front wheels struck, pitching him against the post and popping open his eyes.

Bouncing rapidly, the craft shuddered across thirty yards of grass, and stopped.

Mr. Martin tugged the goggles onto his forehead and smiled at Mackenzie. "Well done, boy," he said. "What did you think of that?"

"It was incredible," Mackenzie said. "Thank you very much." When he saw the airman start to step down from his perch, he quickly added, "Mr. Martin, I saw those thieves. Mr. Brittner and the shoeshines were hiding in some bushes."

"Here? On the flight? I never saw anything."

Slipping off the wing, Mackenzie handed his goggles to the Birdman. "Just before you turned around." As the others circled them, Mackenzie explained how he had tried to get Mr. Martin's attention. Turning to his father, he said, "I saw Mr. Brittner. He's hiding out there."

Hearing that news, all four men spoke at once.

"Are you certain it was them, son?"

"Do you think they know they were seen, sir?" Mr. Shannon asked.

"If they did," Joseph Bear said, "they'll likely make a run for it."

"We were never high off the ground or going very fast," Mr. Martin said, slowly unbuttoning his jacket. "If they looked up at all they'd have seen Mackenzie as much as he saw them."

"We'll have to get the police," Mackenzie's father said. "Could you do that, Mr. Martin?"

"It might take a couple of hours to get any number of police out here, even if I fly to the fairgrounds and hail a ride downtown."

"We could do it," Joseph Bear said, "Junior and me and the others."

"We have a train to board this evening, Mr. Martin," Mr. Shannon cautioned. "We'll need all the time we've got before then to crate up your aeroplane. If we're not on that train, we may miss our connections to Chicago."

"Could you find that bluff, again, Mackenzie?" his

father asked. "If that's where they're hiding, they must not be visible from the ground, only from above."

"I don't want to leave our friends in the lurch," Mr. Martin said. "Everyone's been very good to us here."

"These boys are good trackers," Joseph Bear said. "Finding the path of a loaded wagon is nothing once you've trailed a deer for a couple of miles."

Mackenzie felt Junior tug at his sleeve and he stepped back from the men to join him.

"What was it like up there?" Junior asked. "Did you go very high?"

"Mr. Martin said we weren't as high as the buildings downtown."

"Did you ever fly overtop of someone?"

"Yes! More than once. I'd see them first, when we were still a good distance off. Then I could tell when they'd heard the engine. They'd stop and try to figure out where the noise was coming from. They'd turn all the way around, sometimes more than once! Then they'd look up and see us and lift their hand to shield their eyes. After that they'd stand like they were frozen to the spot until we'd long passed over."

"Weren't you scared you'd fall off the wing? Or get blown off?"

"I was holding on so tightly I'm sure a tornado couldn't have torn me away."

"It might've crashed. You could get hurt pretty bad."

Mackenzie laughed. "You could lose your grip, too. Or your horse might trip and fall. That could be worse." He turned back to the men. "What are they talking about, now?"

"I said," – it was Joseph speaking – "me and these guys could get them for you."

Everyone stopped talking as the horsemen rode up to the aeroplane. They wore oiled leather chaps, some with fringes down the side, brightly coloured shirts and tall, wide-brimmed felt hats. Riding high in their saddles, their backs were straight and the high heels of their boots solidly snugged into metal stirrups. Cowboys, Mackenzie thought, real cowboys.

Joseph called to the men. "You fellas got time to round up a few outlaws? You know how to chase down a wagon."

"Outlaws?" one of the men asked. "Who? What've they done?"

"That Mr. Brittner and his shoeshines that everyone's talking about. They're holed up not far from here. The boy here spotted them when he was up for an aeroplane ride."

"Which boy got a ride? You, Junior?"

"Naw. The only time Junior flies is when he gets bucked from a horse."

Mackenzie looked over at Junior. He was smiling but he put his head down and didn't reply.

Joseph caught Mackenzie's father's eye and waved him over. "They'll do it," he said. "But it'll take them a while to get ready. How about you boys ride out that way. It shouldn't be too hard to follow their trail."

"May I go?" Mackenzie asked.

"They'll be fine," Joseph said. "You track them, Junior, but don't get too close. You're there to watch. You're a scout, not a warrior."

"I know." Junior tugged on his hat. "He'll need a horse."

"He can take mine," Joseph said. "She won't hurry but she'll get you there." Turning to Mackenzie, he asked, "Do you need a saddle?"

Mackenzie wondered. He'd never ridden bareback outside a corral. But putting on a saddle and adjusting the stirrups would take time. He could tell Junior wanted to get going. "No," he said. "I don't need one."

Mackenzie's father looked at him closely. "You're sure? You won't be able to go very fast."

"We won't," Junior said.

"Okay."

Mackenzie and Junior slipped past the men who were now dismounted and milling about Joseph Bear, peppering him with questions. When they reached the wagon, Junior untied the horses. Taking the reins for a tall, dark brown mare, Mackenzie watched the other boy spring to the back of his horse.

"Climb in the back of the buggy," Junior said. "It won't be so far to get on."

Hoisting himself into the cluttered bed, Mackenzie spied Albert's telescope. He picked it up and slid it into his trousers pocket. Then he put on his cap.

The mare swung her head to look at him. Patting

her neck, Mackenzie said, "I won't ask you to go fast, and you don't try to buck me."

"She won't," Junior said. "Her name is Cloud."

Mackenzie threw his leg over the horse's back and immediately clamped his knees against her sides. She was a sturdy horse and all he had to do, he knew, was keep himself centred over her broad back. He reached forward and picked up her lead.

"Mackenzie!"

Turning, Mackenzie found Mr. Martin walking toward him.

"You're off on another adventure, I hear." Mr. Martin said. "I wanted to say goodbye."

"When are you leaving?"

"As soon as Mr. Shannon finishes his inspection. I'm going to fly to the railway siding. He'll meet me there. We'll find someone to notify the police, then box up the aeroplane and be on our way. Thank you again for finding my model." He held up his arm to shake Mackenzie's hand.

"You're welcome. Thanks for the ride!"

Junior clicked his tongue, dug his heels gently into his horse's sides and both animals ambled off in the direction of the wagon trail.

Before they dipped into a gully, Mackenzie twisted back toward the men. They had gathered around Joseph's buggy and seemed to be taking things from the boxes and leather bags in the back. The men were calling to each other and laughing. What did they need to do to get ready? Mackenzie wondered. What was so funny about chasing a gang of crooks?

Once on the trail, the boys rode side by side, Junior swaying in time with his horse's rhythm but Mackenzie sitting more stiffly, bouncing on Cloud's back. He missed the stirrups he was used to bracing his feet into.

"How far are they?" Junior asked, peering down at the rutted tracks. "Do you know which bluff you saw them in?"

"It could be a mile, no further. Things look different from the air. It was big, though, not just a couple of trees."

"We'll watch for any signs of wagon wheels leaving the trail," Junior said. "What did these men do?"

"They robbed a lot of houses and sold what they found. They captured a friend and me for awhile, too. Do you want to know how they did it?"

"Sure," Junior said, skipping his eyes from one side of the track to the other.

Ten minutes later, when Mackenzie was getting to the part where he and Jin saw the salamanders, Junior pulled back on the reins. "There! See where the grass is packed down?" He stopped his horse. "And there, the branches of that bush are broken." Swinging his arm out in the direction the wagon had gone, Junior pointed at a bluff nestled into a little gully.

"That might be it," Mackenzie said. "What should we do?"

"We'll make a big circle, starting by going away

from them, and then coming back around. We should not talk anymore. And keep Cloud behind me."

It wasn't long before they lost sight of the bluff. After a few minutes of what seemed like wandering to Mackenzie, Junior led them behind some trees and into a little valley. Dismounting, he reached to tie his horse's reins to a bush. Mackenzie did the same as a family of swallows burst from behind the wall of yellowing leaves. Drawing closer, Junior whispered, "That bluff is about a quarter mile from here. Keep your head down. They might be watching out."

Junior started up the hillside then went down on hands and knees. The boys crawled together to look over the rim of the valley.

That's it, Mackenzie thought. How did Junior know where it was? He pulled the telescope from his pocket and focused on the bluff. Except for the poplar leaves fluttering weakly in the heat, the bush looked still and empty. Slowly, he scanned the glass lens from one end of the bluff to the other. "Aha," he murmured, smiling.

"What do you see?"

"Someone's moving about in there. Mr. Brittner, I think. Maybe all three of them. Now they're really jumping around."

"That's why."

Mackenzie lowered the telescope and saw a cloud of dust sailing toward them from near where Mr. Brittner's gang had left the trail. With the horses spread side by side across the prairie, the riders didn't seem to be in a rush.

Suddenly, a team and wagon charged out of the bush, heading south. Mackenzie quickly found them in the glass. "Bauer's driving. He's really whipping them! Mr. Brittner's hanging on for dear life. Fletcher must be in the back. There he is, sitting in the box! I can see him looking over the side. He's yelling something at Bauer."

"Here they come!" Junior cried. "They're riding now! They flushed them out like a spooked partridge."

"Do you want to try this?" Mackenzie asked, holding out the telescope.

When Junior shook his head, Mackenzie raised the glass toward the horsemen. The figures filling the lens wore leather leggings and feathers stuck in headbands. Red and white and black paint covered their faces and bare chests. Urging on his wild-eyed horse with whooping shouts, each man clutched a rifle in his hand.

What's going on? Mackenzie wondered. "Those are Indians," he said. "What happened to the cowboys?"

"Take another look." Junior laughed. "Don't you recognize them?"

Mackenzie kept the telescope on the riders. "No."

"They're the same ones who were in the Wild West Show. Cowboys or Indians, they don't care. Watch what happens now. You don't need that. They're close enough. Those men in the wagon don't have a chance."

Laying the telescope on the grass, Mackenzie saw the first riders pull even with Bauer and Mr. Brittner. After racing to catch up, the horses easily kept pace with the wagon. As calmly as if they were standing on a shooting range, the horsemen levelled their guns at the robbers. Bauer didn't let up but kept lashing the reins over the horses' backs.

Mackenzie checked Fletcher again. He's got the gun! Trying to steady his arms against the side of the bouncing wagon, the shoeshine aimed at the nearest rider. He thinks he can scare them off, Mackenzie thought.

A horseman charged up behind the wagon, swinging his open lariat over his head. Whipping out his arm, the rider released the lasso which sailed across the wagon and dropped like a hoop over Fletcher's arms. The rider spun the rope around the horn of his saddle, and pulled back on the reins.

His arms bound tightly to his chest, Fletcher slid on his back along the bed of the wagon and dropped like a sack of flour onto the ground.

"Crackers!" Mackenzie cried. "That Indian's good with a lariat!"

"That's my brother," Junior said, beaming. "He can lasso anything."

A shot ran out. A puff of white smoke flew away from the barrel of an Indian rifle. Another shot! A third!

"What are they doing?" Mackenzie watched in horror as another two rifles blasted in the direction of the wagon. "They don't need to kill them!" Then, "Oh. Blanks. Like at the Wild West Show."

"It worked," Junior said.

Bauer hauled back on the reins as an Indian swooped in to grab the bridle of one of the wagon's horses.

Was it an Indian? Mackenzie wondered as he and Junior stood up. Or a cowboy? He stared at the horsemen who had surrounded the thieves. Which is which?

Scrambling down the hill, the boys untied their horses' leads.

"I'll give you a hand," Junior said. "It takes anyone awhile before he can jump bareback onto a horse the size of Cloud." Bending his knees, he cupped his fingers between his legs. With that leg up, Mackenzie easily sprang to the horse's back.

Riding out of the valley a few moments later, the boys met one of the bare-chested riders coming to see them. The man was grinning and his pale skin glistened with sweat.

"What a ride! Did you boys see all that? Junior, your father wants you and your friend to get back to where that aeroplane was. We're going to tie those three up like the ornery steers they are and make them tell us what they did with their loot. Their wagon was empty. Then a couple of the boys will drive them into Saskatoon. More than likely the Mounties will send out a patrol to meet them."

Mackenzie took a last look at the wagon. If the three robbers had noticed him, they didn't let on and he had no desire to get any closer. Junior clicked his tongue. Mackenzie just had time to clamp his legs against Cloud's flanks before the two horses trotted off toward town.

THE LITTLE MEADOW where the aeroplane had taken off and landed was deserted except for Joseph's buggy and the two men sitting side by side on its seat. The place looks sad and empty, Mackenzie thought, like the fairgrounds will when the Exhibition is packed up and gone.

"How did you make out?" Mackenzie's father called.

"They're captured!" Mackenzie pulled up beside the wagon. "Mr. Brittner and the shoeshines tried to make a run for it, but they were too slow. Even then they didn't stop until they were shot at."

"They got to shoot their guns?" Joseph said. "They'll be happy about that. I knew they'd catch them. Where are those boys?"

"They're bringing the robbers back in the wagon." Jumping to the ground, Mackenzie rubbed Cloud's forehead.

"Joseph is being very generous," Mackenzie's father said. "He's going to let us use his horse. We'll put a saddle on her and you can ride behind me."

"Bring her around to the back of the buggy, Junior," Joseph said. "Brush her down before you put on her saddle."

"Then we'll leave," Mackenzie's father said. "I don't want to make your mother wait any longer. She'll be worried enough already. And she'll want lots of time to hear your stories."

Mackenzie watched Junior lead away Cloud. I never told him the rest of what happened, he thought. "When will I see Junior again?" he asked.

"Soon. I'm going to ask Mr. Arnold if we can stable Cloud with Rose for a few days. Joseph is coming back into town next week. He's going to buy a new saddle at Allwood's with some of his earnings from the show. They'll drop by then. Now let's go lend a hand with Cloud."

As they walked toward the Bears, Mackenzie felt his father's arm slip onto his shoulder. He was glad his father had been there to see him fly and to chase the robbers. But he was ready to tell his mother everything, too.

The Daily Phoenix

FRIDAY, AUGUST 9, 1912

SASKATOON KNOWN AROUND THE WORLD

Wonder City of West Still Booming

It would appear that Saskatoon is known all over the world as a place where money can be made from the wise purchase and speedy sale of land.

What better sign could there be of all this money-making than the spectacular rise in the number of land agents in our bustling city. While four years ago there were fewer than ten agents, at the latest count conducted by *The Daily Phoenix* newspaper just this week, over 250 men were being kept busy handling the demand for lots. It is no surprise that Saskatoon has the reputation as the greatest example of town building in the history of the world!

According to Albert B. Crawley, proprietor of ABC Land Sales, the latest trend in our building boom is for locals who have built their fortunes to spend it buying more property in our city.

"Saskatoon is still the Wonder City of the West," Mr. Crawley said. "There is no reason to think that our magic growth in buildings and people will not continue long into the future."

CHAPTER SIX
Saturday, August 10, 1912

WITH ONE HAND SLIDING ALONG THE bridge railing, Mackenzie gazed down at the people bathing in the shallows near the bank. Each day that the weather stayed hot, more families appeared at the river. I hope, he thought, they'll have a real house to live in when winter comes.

At the end of the bridge, Mackenzie turned toward Chinatown. Deep in his trousers pocket he fingered the red ticket. There must have been a perfectly good reason, his mother had told him, for the laundry to have been closed on Friday. But surely today, she said, Mr. Lee would be there, Mackenzie could pick up the package and his father would have a clean shirt to wear to church on Sunday.

Mackenzie wasn't so sure. If Jin and his father were gone, Mr. Lee wouldn't be able to run the laundry.

Who would do all the washing? The ironing? Who would make the deliveries?

Looking ahead to the laundry building, Mackenzie was surprised to see the "CLOSED" sign had been taken down. When he spotted Albert sitting at the edge of the boardwalk, his cast cradled in his lap, he was even more surprised.

"What are you doing here?" he asked.

"Waiting for my father," Albert said. "He's inside." Smiling, he looked up at Mackenzie. "You were busy after I left yesterday. Flew an aeroplane. Rode bareback with some Indians chasing down a gang of robbers. That's what I heard."

"It wasn't exactly like that." Laughing, Mackenzie sat down beside his friend. "But do you want to know something, Albert? Madame La Claire was right. She said somebody close to your family would find the jewellery and that person would go on an exciting trip."

"*You* were the one she was talking about. Of course. She *can* predict the future.

"Not only that. Remember when you were pestering her on Broadway and she told you that life isn't simple? That the truth is hidden by illusions? She was right about that, too, like you said. Mr. Brittner wasn't who he pretended to be. And I saw Indians who were really cowboys. And cowboys who were really Indians. And sometimes they shot people, but with blanks in their guns."

There might be more things, too, Mackenzie knew. The biggest illusion of all he hadn't yet figured out.

"I always knew she could do it," Albert said.

"Don't give me that guff." Mackenzie wasn't about to believe anything Albert said about the fortune teller. "What's your father doing in there?"

"Thanking that Chinaman friend of yours for helping to foil Brittner and his gang."

"Jin doesn't live here anymore, remember? I told you he's gone back to Vancouver."

"I thought so. My mother said it wasn't Jim, it was a new boy who delivered her laundry this morning."

"Jin. Not Jim." Mackenzie frowned. They've really gone, he decided. Mr. Lee already has found people to replace them.

"I stopped at that fly contest on my way here," Albert said. "What a muddle!"

"Who won?"

"I didn't stick around to find out. There must have been a hundred kids there, half of them girls and the rest little tykes holding their mothers' hands. They were lined up halfway down the block. Each one had a glass jar with an inch or two of dead flies at the bottom. Dr. McKay and three assistants were counting the bottles, one fly at a time. It was going to take hours. I guess you were right, Mack. It was a stupid idea. Except we could have made some money selling our flies to one of those kids. I think that's what Four-Eyes and Badger Breath did."

Albert's always running into Eunice and Ruth Anne, Mackenzie thought. I wonder if *he's* going to be one of their boyfriends soon. Someone's always first, Mother says. I'll be darned if it'll be me.

"I'm picking up some laundry," Mackenzie said, getting to his feet. He held out his arm for Albert. "Come with me."

Mr. Lee and Albert's father were deep in conversation at the counter when Mackenzie opened the door. At the sound of the bell jangling, they looked up.

"Mack!" Mr. Crawley held out his hand. "I want to thank you for tracking down our valuables. I always knew you were a clever lad."

"Thank you."

"I've been telling Mr. Lee what a brave boy he has working for him. That Jim."

"It's Jin, I think, Mr. Crawley."

Albert's father paused. "Hmm," he said.

And he doesn't work here any longer, Mackenzie wanted to add.

"Mr. Davis will pay later," Mr. Lee said, handing Mackenzie his parcel.

Mackenzie wanted to ask Mr. Lee about Jin but he knew it would be rude to inquire now.

"Albert," Mr. Crawley said, "don't go wandering off with Mack. Mr. Lee and I have to talk about a building he may want to buy from me. Then we'll go back to my office."

That's really why Mr. Crawley's here, Mackenzie thought. Mr. Lee is wealthy enough to buy a building. He turned and whispered to Albert. "The Chinese aren't so different, see? Your father knows that." He continued toward the door.

Outside, Mackenzie stopped so that three women walking arm in arm could pass on the boardwalk. Now that the Exhibition is over, he thought, there aren't as many people on the streets. If Jin was delivering laundry today, it wouldn't be so hard to stay out of their way.

A strange boy carrying two green laundry bags on a pole resting on his shoulder stepped out from beside the laundry. Startled, Mackenzie backed up. The boy glanced his way and would have continued down the street except a voice called to him in Chinese. He stopped and a moment later someone familiar joined him.

"Jin!"

The boy beside him was taller and heavier than Jin. "This is my brother, Shen," he said. Then, "And this is Mackenzie, my friend."

Shen dropped the bags and shook Mackenzie's hand. "Thank you for taking care of Jin," he said. "My whole family thanks you." He reached down and in one smooth movement brought the pole to his shoulder.

I could never do that, Mackenzie thought.

"I have to go," Shen said. "I am not as fast as Jin yet. I do not know where all the stores are." He set off toward First Avenue.

"Where have you been?" Mackenzie asked. "When I came here yesterday the laundry was closed. I thought your uncle had sent you away."

"I was wrong about my uncle. He worried about me when I was gone for so long that night. But he said I was right to try to help you."

"Why was the laundry closed, then?"

Grinning, Jin pointed after Shen. "All of my family has arrived! My father insisted that he and I go to the station to meet them. My uncle was so excited he had to come too. When we were back at the laundry he wanted to hear all the news of his old friends in Vancouver from my mother. He said it wouldn't hurt anyone to wait a few hours to get their clean clothes."

"But before that, you used to think he was angry with you all the time. You were never fast enough for him."

"I know. My mother said that even after I showed him I could do the deliveries he was afraid for me. That's why he was grouchy all the time. He didn't want me to get hurt."

"Albert told me that some other boy delivered their laundry. Was that –"

"Shen! My uncle says that he is learning very fast. Next week I will show him more places. When he is ready, he will do that and I will help my mother iron the clothes. That is better for me."

"Wouldn't you rather be outside delivering things?" Mackenzie asked. "Ironing's a girl's job."

Jin frowned. "There is something I must tell you," he said.

"Sure. Okay. I've got stories to tell you, too. Did you hear about the Birdman and me?"

"No. But this is different, Mackenzie. You might not like what I say."

"Are you still moving? That's about the only thing I can think of I don't want you to say."

"I told you already," Jin said, "that when my uncle paid for my family to come here, we were all supposed to travel together. Then my sister became ill and only my father and I could come." He paused. "At first my uncle was not happy to see me. He wanted a boy to do the deliveries."

"You mean an older boy," Mackenzie said. "Like your brother, Shen. But you showed you're strong enough."

"It is not about being strong enough. It is about what is proper. My father did not want to upset my uncle after he had paid so much money to bring us to Saskatoon. But he knew it would be a few weeks before my brother arrived. He convinced my uncle that I could do the work and that no one would know."

"What's there to know?"

"Wait. I am not finished. Delivering laundry is hard work but I was happy to do it to help my family. I did not know anybody in Saskatoon so I did not mind pretending for awhile. My father said I should not tell anyone. I should not bring shame on my uncle. He said that once my brother started delivering laundry everyone would forget that I did it for a short time."

How had Jin been pretending? Mackenzie wondered. What was he really like?

"My brother is here now," Jin went on quickly, "so I'm telling you everything. I am not a boy, Mackenzie. I am a girl."

Mackenzie remembered what it was like at the end of the aeroplane flight and the ground was rushing up to smack him. He felt like he was about to crash. "Do you mean...?" he began, then faltered.

With nothing more to say, Jin watched Mackenzie.

Mackenzie stared back. Jin looks the same as he always did, he thought. His face is the same, and his hair trimmed over his ears. He's wearing the same blue outfit that looks like pyjamas. Was this another illusion like the fortune teller predicted?

"You're a girl? Why wouldn't you just tell me?"

"I explained that. My family did not want people to know that a girl was doing the work of a boy. I could not tell anyone. If I had, my uncle would have demanded his money and put us on the train back to Vancouver."

"You don't look like a girl."

"Soon I will. Mother brought my dresses in her trunk. The next time you see me I will be wearing one."

Mackenzie's head was spinning now. He liked Jin, when he was a boy. "I thought you were my friend."

"You *are* my friend."

"All my friends are boys."

Jin giggled. Mackenzie gaped. It sounded like a girl's laughter now.

"Girls and boys can be friends," Jin said.

"I don't know about that," Mackenzie said. If Jin is my friend now, he thought, he – she! – has to be my *girl*friend.

"I liked the things we used to do together, like when you tripped Fletcher. And I tried to save you." And the times I carried your bags. Jin was stronger than me, Mackenzie remembered, and never complained about how much the pole hurt. And she's a girl.

"I knew something was odd about you," Mackenzie said. "Albert told me it was because you were Chinese." But that was wrong, he thought. It was how Jin treated Nellie. "Most boys don't like to spend all that time with baby sisters."

"That won't change," Jin said. "We're going to be different from each other, but that doesn't mean we can't be friends."

Mackenzie thought about riding bareback and tracking the robbers' wagon with his new friend Junior. He thought about Stanley, his friend who worked for Henry Lavallée and got bigger and stronger every day. Albert, his best friend, was a few yards away in the laundry probably thinking up his next cockamamy scheme for them. They were all different and he didn't want any of them to change one bit. I guess Jin can be different too, Mackenzie thought.

"All right," he said, "I'll still be your friend."

"And I will be yours," Jin said. "Now it is time for *your* story, Mackenzie. What happened with you and the Birdman?"

The Daily Phoenix

SATURDAY, AUGUST 10, 1912

THE LAST FLIGHT OF THE BIRDMAN

Police Capture Renegade Merchant Behind Crime Spree

The last flight of the Birdman left the ground late on Friday afternoon and set off a startling string of events that ended with the capture of outlaw businessman Cornelius Brittner. On board Mr. Martin's aeroplane was a young lad who spied Brittner and his accomplices hiding not far from the city.

Upon landing the craft, Mr. Martin helped organize a posse of cowboys to round up the thieves before they could make their getaway. These cowboys were none other than the local horsemen who for the past week had dressed in various roles for performances of the 101 Ranch Wild West Show. Rigged up as Indian warriors, the men of the posse quickly surprised and ensnared the gang of robbers. Soon they discovered the suspects had buried all their stolen loot with the intention of sneaking across the American border and returning for their stashes at some future date.

Although a complete list of items found in the caches and at Brittner's store has not yet been compiled, Chief Dunning is confident that most if not all of the stolen property can be returned to its owners.

PHOTO: MEGAN BOCKING

About the Author

BORN IN BRITISH COLUMBIA, Dave Glaze grew up in Alberta, Ontario and Saskatchewan. At various times he has made his living as a journalist, a social worker, a landscaper and a lumber mill worker, but for most of his working life he's been a teacher and teacher-librarian in elementary schools.

The Last Flight of the Birdman is the second novel in the Mackenzie Davis Files series which began with *The Light-Fingered Gang*. Dave Glaze is also the author of the Pelly stories: *Pelly, Waiting for Pelly* and the upcoming *Save Pelly*.

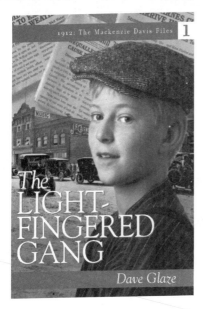

MEMBRE DU GROUPE SCABRINI

Québec, Canada
2007